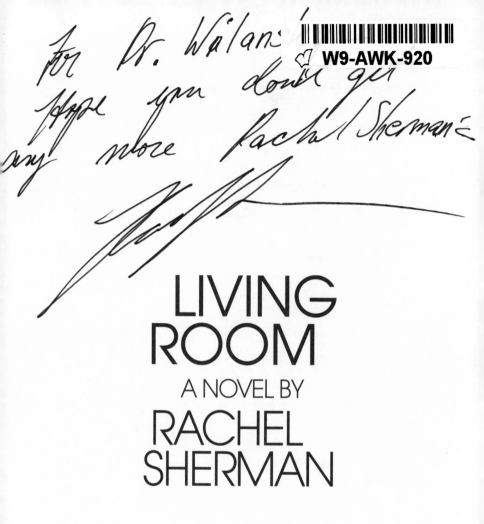

For Dr. Walan...
Hope you don't get
any more   Rachel Sherman

LIVING
ROOM
A NOVEL BY
RACHEL
SHERMAN

 **OPEN CITY BOOKS**

New York

Printed in the United States of America

FIRST EDITION

Design by Nick Stone
Cover photograph by Haley Richter, *Naomi*, 2007
Author photograph by Laura Rose

Library of Congress Control Number: 2009933419

OPEN CITY BOOKS
270 Lafayette Street
New York, NY 10012
www.opencity.org

ISBN-13: 978-1-890447-53-3

09 10 11 12 13 14   10 9 8 7 6 5 4 3 2 1

For Mike

1.

Abby walks Jenna toward her house, across the high school fields. She looks out at the road that runs next to the grass, making sure that no teachers are around.

The sky is gray and it looks like rain but Abby leads Jenna slowly. Her house is so close to the school she can hear school sports games—the yells from the chalk-against-blackboard–like squeak of the metal bleachers—even with the windows closed. She always tries to make the time from the school to her house last as long as she can.

Abby looks over at Jenna, walking forward against the wind. A flash of the bright, shiny pink lining of Jenna's bomber jacket peeks out while she brushes back her hair with her hand. It is getting colder, and Abby folds her army jacket around herself. The wind picks up, then seems to let go.

Abby can hear the bell ring, and looks at her watch. It is the second class she is skipping today, but for good reason. Last period (gym) she spent in the girls' bathroom, with Jenna, getting her eyebrows plucked.

Abby touches the new thin line of hair above her eyes as they enter the woods at the edge of the field.

"Don't touch too much," Jenna says, getting close to Abby, pulling her hand away from herself. "You'll get zits."

Jenna knows these things. Her mother is an aesthetician. Last period, in the girls' bathroom, Abby looked into Jenna's green colored contacts while Jenna bit her lower lip and stared above Abby's eyes. Up that close Abby could see where the mascara had congealed on Jenna's eyelashes.

Jenna had drawn lines beneath each of Abby's eyebrows with blue eyeliner to guide her.

"You have such fucking long eyebrow hairs!" Jenna laughed.

It felt like tiny pinpricks, how Abby imagines acupuncture feels. It felt good to sit and let pretty Jenna Marino with her down-turned mouth and her soft brown hair, her perfectly shaped eyebrows and her mother's special tweezers, pluck her away.

Now they are going home for Jenna to finish the job. Now it is time for wax.

At the small opening in the woods, there are old tackling dummies, just behind the trees, forgotten. There is something about being in the woods, looking out from the edge of them, onto the field, down to the school, that makes Abby feel safe.

"So," Abby says as they stand lighting cigarettes, out of sight. She knows it is inevitable, so she takes a breath and says it: "There's a guy that lives with us, a housekeeper kind of, from Sweden."

Someone honks their horn from the parking lot. "What?" Jenna says.

"It's called an au pair. He is. But he's only nineteen. His name is Jorgen," Abby says, pronouncing his name the way he does: *U-rine*.

"U-RINE?" Jenna laughs, inhaling.

"That's how you say it, not how you spell it," Abby says. She points ahead to the small opening in the woods.

Jenna exhales a big, long plume. "So what does U-RINE do?"

"Um, just cleans our house," Abby says, thinking, suddenly, how strange it sounds. "And does our laundry."

Abby watches as Jenna's face scrunches up, her beautiful skin wrinkling around her nose. She laughs, and Abby does too.

"U-RINE," Jenna says, making a face. "Is he hot?" She French-inhales her last drag and then drops her cigarette, stomping it.

Abby exhales, shakes her head no, putting her butt out on a tree trunk. They both rub their fingers with pine needles as they walk to cover up their smoky smell.

"Come on," Jenna says. "Not even a little?"

"No," Abby says, pointing to her house once they are past the line of bushes that separates her lawn from the next. She feels like Jenna might not believe her.

"You have a really nice lawn," Jenna says as they walk across it.

Abby walks ahead and opens the back door that leads into the kitchen. She watches Jenna's face as she enters.

Jorgen is at the counter, making chicken—plain, the way her mother taught him. He parts his hair to the side and has acne and a thick accent. He has been here for almost two months, since August.

Abby's mother had to teach Jorgen to cook because he only knows from meatballs.

"Hi Jorgen," Abby says. "This is Jenna."

Abby watches Jorgen as he looks past her, to Jenna. She turns around and sees that Jenna is leaning over, taking off her shoes, and that the way she is leaning makes her breast show, the cup of her bra to the side so you can see her nipple.

All she really knows about Jorgen is that he sleeps with the fluorescent overhead lights on in the basement and that he told her and her parents, one night at dinner, that his best friend back home is in a wheelchair.

Now here he is, looking at Jenna's breast.

"Let's go upstairs," Abby says, walking past Jorgen out of the kitchen.

"Do you want a schnack?" Jorgen asks.

"No," Abby calls back, making sure that Jenna is right behind her.

The au pairs have been around forever. There had been a new girl each year, shipped from Sweden, always the same age, always blond and ready.

Au pairs were good for sitting and modeling on the couch when she did her art class assignments, drawing their ears and noses, and good for teaching her how to knit. Sometimes they were sweet, and then Abby felt bad that she liked her house better in the summers, between them, when it was just her and her mom and dad.

She liked some girls more than others. Then, this year, Abby's mother decided to get a male au pair.

"You might like a man better," her mother told her.

Her mother had called her into her room and moved her feet under the covers, to the side, so that Abby could sit next to her on the bed. She told Abby she was making sure to pick an unattractive one because otherwise it would make Abby uncomfortable.

From her bed, her mother picked Jorgen. She showed Abby his picture: a plain boy with darkish blond hair swept to the side. He looked like a dork in his red tracksuit (the au pairs always had shiny tracksuits, flip-flops with pointed plastic on the bottom so that it cushioned their feet, and they all loved Nike but said it wrong, without the long "e," like "bike").

Abby shrugged. She didn't care, then. She didn't even think of him until he arrived in the same red tracksuit, smelling strange, his English worse than the others', one of his two front teeth a little brown.

Jorgen disgusted her. He said his name was pronounced "urine." He didn't know what he was saying, and Abby didn't tell him.

Now Abby leads Jenna up to her room, and as soon as the door is closed Jenna begins to laugh.

"That guy is such a fucking loser!" she says. Her white shirt slips down again so Abby can see the top of her lacy bra.

"I know," Abby says.

Abby sits on her bed and watches Jenna look around her room. Abby sees that she is staring at two framed pictures of Japanese cutouts her parents brought back from a trip they took without her.

"Lay down on your bed," Jenna says, taking a white plastic jar from her silver bag and getting up to sit beside her.

"Why?" Abby asks.

"The wax," Jenna says. "What do you think?"

Abby had forgotten about the wax. Jenna is here for a reason.

Jenna spreads the wax above Abby's lip with a thin wooden stick. It is the cold kind, Jenna says, easier. She wonders if Jenna always carries wax around, just waiting for the next hairy girl to clean.

Abby closes her eyes and Jenna counts to three, then rips the stuff from her skin. This time it really does hurt.

"Fuck!" Abby says.

"Holy shit!" Jenna laughs, holding the wax up to show the hairs that have come off with it, tangled inside the goo like a web. "You're like a man!"

Abby doesn't say anything. She touches her new, smooth lip and feels herself blush.

Still, she is grateful. Jenna Marino, the girl with the young mother who all the teachers recognized in her face and in her laugh, is at her house. "You're just like your mother," said her English, Spanish, and math teachers—the classes that Jenna and Abby shared. Her mother, everyone learned early last year, had her when she was a senior at their very school. Her mother walked down the same halls, unlocked the same lockers.

"Do you think Jorgen is a virgin?" Jenna says, getting up to throw the wax in the garbage. "Sit up," she says, coming back to sit next to her and taking one of her arms. She scoops the wax with the stick and begins to spread it from Abby's wrist to her elbow.

Abby watches. She has not thought about Jorgen's virginity before.

"Yes," she says.

"That's pathetic," Jenna says, then turns back to Abby. "I mean, he's a fucking guy!"

"Yeah, I know," Abby says.

Jenna laughs, her mouth open, and Abby smiles. Jenna rips the hair from both of Abby's arms, then holds the skin down, patting it, taking out lotion from her bag and rubbing it on her gently.

"Great!" Jenna says. "Come here!"

Abby follows Jenna to her own mirror. Both of their faces hardly fit inside the circle.

"Look!" Jenna says, pointing to her red upper lip and raw-looking eyebrows. "The swelling will go down. It looks SO much better already!"

Abby looks and sees. She compares her own eyes (they are smaller), her lips (they are bigger) and her teeth (they are whiter) to Jenna's. She can hear Jorgen banging pots downstairs. Jenna smiles so her dimple shows.

Surprisingly, Abby does not feel ugly next to Jenna. No, she sees, she is even a little pretty. Just different, darker, pointed. Her smile is less wide, but she is just as hairless.

"See?" Jenna smirks. "Thank God you agreed," she says, because it had been Jenna who approached her in the bathroom, told her she could do something for all that hair.

Abby hadn't asked, but now she sees. It is what she has been waiting for. She watches in the mirror as Jenna turns and licks her on the cheek quickly, then looks into her mirror eyes and laughs again.

At night, once she is in bed, Abby imagines having a good-looking au pair. A light blond one. He can wear a tracksuit, but it has to be black. He wears the au pair sandals, but only when he is in the house.

His name is Lars, like that German foreign exchange student they had last year at school.

"Can I get you a snack, Abby?" he asks her when they are alone.

They eat potato chips together at the kitchen table and laugh and punch each other lightly on the arm.

She imagines Jenna coming over, and Lars ignoring her, only looking at Abby.

When Jenna tries to get Lars's attention, he hardly notices; when she shows her boob, he looks away.

He is a different kind of au pair, a different kind of man. Specially picked to come to her house for a year.

Lars lets her draw him and drives her places, but mostly, he is her friend. He is special, better, not like that.

2.

Headie knows she has to answer the door or people will think she's dead. She is old and people think things like that, even when there is no reason. Recently she had gotten sick, which made it worse. People calling, acting as if they just wanted to chat. This new illness has her inside her house except to go to synagogue and get her hair done once a week. Outside, the doctor says, are germs.

"Who is it?" she says as loudly as she can. She had been on her way to the bathroom, on her hands and knees, when the doorbell rang.

"Delivery," a man's voice says. "For Mrs. Headra Goldstein."

Slowly, on all fours, she turns around for the door.

"What is it?" Headie asks. She does not want him to give her something she does not want.

"I don't know, ma'am."

"Who's it from?" she asks.

"A Mr. Jeffrey Schecter," the man says. "From New York."

The voice sounds impressed. It should be, she thinks. Her son Jeffrey is a lawyer.

Headie pushes herself to her feet, her head up last. She feels dizzy as she wraps her bathrobe around her and unlocks and opens the door. A cool breeze comes in that she can feel under her bathrobe. A short man in brown shorts and matching uniform shirt holds a box on her doorstep.

"It looks like a computer, ma'am," he says.

The man has a blond buzz cut and is clean-shaven. Headie wants to invite him in. She could defrost one of the bagels that Jeffrey brought up the last time he visited from New York. They could sit at the table and talk about the man's job, wife, and children. Headie could listen, pour him coffee.

Instead Headie signs the slip, thanking the man. She watches as he walks back to his brown truck, into the gray day. He is short but proportioned. She looks at his thick calves and imagines taking out a picture of her younger self to show him.

Headie closes the door and carries the package to the kitchen table, walking slowly on her crumpled toes. The package is too small to be a computer, she thinks, and too light. Perhaps Jeffrey sent her a new dish rack, all folded up. This would be nice, Headie thinks, but unnecessary.

She takes a knife from the drawer and slides it in between the cardboard. Then she sees them: the people dancing out of the corner of her eye. Men and women at a ball, ignoring her, smiling.

Headie shakes her head and they disappear. She has to open the package quickly; it is past her bath time and there are things to do.

She breaks open the box and undoes the bubble wrap. On top of it is a note.

Enjoy! It says. *Call Millie to help you! Love Jeffrey, Liv, and Abby*

Inside is a flat white device she takes out and opens. Her fifteen-year-old granddaughter, Abby, brought one just like it on her last visit. It is a computer.

Headie's elderly life, six months earlier, had gotten a second wind. Her second husband, Allen, had died five years ago, and it had taken her awhile, but she had become a volunteer librarian. She bought a used red convertible but never put the hood down. She drove to the library and back.

Only a few months ago, Sam Toubin baked her a challah shaped like a heart. He brought it over, and the two widowers sat in Headie's living room in her dead husband's chairs, eating chopped liver on saltines.

But then Headie got sick. And when she felt better, her doctor said that the library had too many germs for her to be there. Sam Toubin fell ill, too, and now she has to stay in her house alone with no one to cook for. She separates the space of the day into meals, vacuuming, reading mystery novels, and more vacuuming. She goes to bed early so that the day will pass.

Headie gets back down on her knees, leaving the computer to sit on the table for now. She takes her bath every day at three. It is almost time—she can feel it. But the bathtub seems so far away. The carpet is an ocean of brown. She still can't tell if she likes the color of the carpet that Allen picked. She thinks about this a lot, looking closely at it as she crawls.

She needs to get to her bath. She can see her big Jean Naté bottle through the open bathroom door down the hall up ahead. The bottle comes up to her waist. Allen gave it to her for her birthday when they first got married. Now it sits on the tiles in the bathroom. Allen always gave her more than what she needed.

The bottle needs refilling. She always keeps it full.

When Headie takes a bubble bath she pours the soap in the cap, then gently empties the cap in the bathwater. She then fills the part of the bottle that she has used up with water before getting out. This has diluted the bubble bath over the years, and now the liquid is only the faintest yellow. It still makes bubbles, though. It is enough.

Headie pauses on the floor, a hallway away from the bathroom. Halfway down the hall, she feels dizzy again. She is tired.

She turns herself on her back and looks up at the ceiling. She rests midway, putting her ear on the brown carpet. It does not sound like anything.

Headie began crawling a few weeks earlier. It suddenly occurred to her when she was down on the floor trying to pick up a piece of lint. Why get up only to sit back down? She wondered why she had never thought of this before.

Headie gets back on her knees, making prints with her hands in the carpet. She will have to vacuum again, striping the pile back to its back-and-forth pattern before bed.

Jean Naté, Jean Naté, she thinks. What the hell does that mean?

She sees the couples dancing again. It started a bit before she began to crawl. The men that she sees always wear tuxes; the women are bright colored dresses, blurs.

Headie knows that this is strange, but she doesn't mind. When she turns her head they always go away.

On Fridays, before Headie and Millie go to synagogue, they stop at the Jewish cemetery and help each other, sister-in-law and sister-in-law, climb to their dead husbands' graves. Headie has lived in the area her entire life—coal-mining northeastern Pennsylvania. Just the other day Millie told her that she read they had the largest population of elderly people in America. It was like the area had aged with Headie—both used to feel so young.

Millie is her second husband's sister. She is heavy and breathes hard. They both have old ankles, and some days it is more difficult for one of them to walk than the other. When they are both having trouble, feet swollen and cramped, one holds the back of the other's coat while she bends down to pick up a rock and places it on top of the stone.

Headie doesn't go to her first husband's grave anymore. Going to Gene's grave is too long of a walk now, and she doesn't want to bother Millie with it. Also, she figures, he is done being prayed for, being dead so long. He died young, leaving her when Jeffrey was still in high school. Her first husband has been prayed for enough.

•

After her bath, Headie crawls in her bathrobe to the kitchen. She pulls herself up in the chair and calls Millie.

"Did you get it?" Millie asks before she can tell her.

"The computer? You knew?" Headie asks.

"Of course," Millie says. "Jeffrey emailed me so that I can help you set it up."

Millie bought her own computer years ago and uses it to write to her children and grandchildren. She has been bragging about it to Headie forever.

On their way to synagogue, the whole car ride is filled with Millie's stories. Headie often puts down the window, even when it is cold (she tells Millie it must be her medicine making her hot), hoping that the wind will drown out her sister-in-law's mouth. Headie likes the feeling of the wind: it makes her think she has a different face than she actually does. The wind feels the same way it did when she was a child, when she was a teenager, and it amazes her that it feels the same way now, even though her face has changed.

Millie always tells her the news of her family: her grandson in law school (he has been divorced once), and her granddaughter just engaged (she goes to a community college). Sometimes Millie asks about Abby and Headie tells her she is fine.

Abby used to send Headie beaded jewelry that she made, which Headie opened and then put in her bag for the synagogue rummage sale. She often felt like giving Abby the jewelry back, telling her she wouldn't wear it. She had done that once before when she gave back a silk scarf that Livia, her daughter-in-law, had given her for Hanukkah. When Headie sent it back to her in the mail with a note explaining that she would never wear it, Jeffrey told her that Livia had cried. Headie's son said that people did not do that, so Headie thanked Abby for the lovely beads and quietly packed them up. Headie wishes she had at least kept one of those bracelets now that Abby no longer makes them, or at least no longer sends them to Headie.

"Wow! A computer!" Millie says over the phone.

"Can you teach me what to do?" Headie says.

"Yes, I'll come over tomorrow."

After Headie gets off the phone she takes out the Fantastik and sprays the computer, then sits down at the table to watch it dry. Sometimes she has energy, out of nowhere. It comes and goes, like the dancers.

She pushes a button on the outside and the computer opens. A sound comes on—the strangest sound. It sounds like the yoga music Livia listened to in the living room, that weird chanting, when they visited once.

Headie presses another button and calls Millie again.

"It's making noise," she says, watching the computer begin to change.

"That's because you turned it on. Now let the thing be until the screen becomes clear," Millie says to her.

The screen is moving fast, a line like a sideways thermometer going up and up in temperature, then disappearing. Small pictures pop up on the side.

"Now, you can't get on the Internet without a service, so tomorrow we'll call up for one, and then you can plug it into the phone jack, and look on the World Wide Web!" Millie says.

She makes it sound so important that after Headie gets off the phone, she is afraid to touch the thing. She watches as the screen dims, then goes black.

At night she wakes up almost every hour to listen, turning her ear in the computer's direction, making sure that it hasn't caught fire or blown up.

The next morning, Millie comes over at nine-thirty, unannounced, her black hair wrapped in a handkerchief.

"I already called the service for you, so you should be online soon," Millie says.

She takes off her coat and puts it on a chair. She is wearing red lipstick and seems very excited.

"Is it so special?" Headie asks. She is dressed in one of the sweaters Livia gave her, with her tan cotton skirt and her white bedroom slippers.

"Oh, Headie, I just worry about you, and I think that some change—something like this—would do you good. It was so thoughtful of Jeffrey to buy it for you."

Millie plugs in wires that Headie didn't even know were there. She picks up the lid and the computer makes its sound again.

"Ooooohhhhmmm," it says.

"Why does it say that?" Headie asks.

"Oh, I don't know," Millie says. She pushes past Headie, then slowly leans down while she holds on to the table. Headie watches as she bends at the knees the way the doctors told them to.

Millie unplugs Headie's phone.

"What are you doing?" Headie asks.

Headie watches as she plugs a wire from the computer into the jack.

"Don't worry," Millie says, "we can take it out."

Millie slowly stands, holding on to the wall and the table. When she is finally up she reaches her hands to touch her back and begins her heavy breathing.

"Oh, Headie," she says. "I feel dizzy now."

"Just sit," Headie says. She has always thought Millie was too dramatic.

Millie sits.

"Do you want water?" Headie says.

"No, I'm fine," Millie says, her face red. "That was so sweet of them to send you this," she says again, as if she hadn't said how nice it was the first time.

"Jeffrey and Livia are thoughtful," Headie says.

Thoughtful Livia. She was not who Headie had expected her son to marry. When he first brought her home they tickled each other on the living room rug, rolling around on the floor together like puppies. Headie could tell that Livia had dressed up to meet her, but that she wasn't wearing a bra.

Jeffrey told Headie on the phone that Livia was from Philadelphia, and that she had studied English. She was a pretty girl, with big, almost black eyes. And a figure. Headie wasn't blind.

"What's she going to do now?" Headie asked her son.

"Maybe teach, or go on to her PhD . . ." he said, "and hopefully marry me!"

Headie had watched Livia and Jeffrey dance at their wedding. Livia looked beautiful, but she was not a good dancer, and this bothered Headie. She wondered if Livia was all talk: if her women's liberation, her non-cooking, non-cleaning, arguing was just a pose. Perhaps underneath she was a prude, and never really pleased Jeffrey the way he deserved. Headie knew what it meant when people did not move well together. She watched her son try to lead Livia at their wedding, and Livia, drunk and out of step, being held up by her nice white gloves.

3.

Livia eats like a fat man. She sets up a sheet like a picnic blanket on the grass of her bedroom floor carpet, laying out her spread from the storage bins she hides in her closet.

Livia is not a fat man. She is not even fat. She is forty-five years old and still in her nightgown at two p.m. on a Thursday, opening the pre-made onion dip and chips and beginning, rubbing her fingers on the sheet in between bites.

She wishes she were hungrier, but she had woken in the middle of the night to eat Ring Dings from her stash and frozen yogurt from the freezer. It was the reason she got up especially late today.

Now she eats, looking out the window into the dull gray day with still-sleepy eyes. There is nothing like onion dip and chips. Nothing.

Livia had tried to get up earlier but her dreams dragged her down. Her reward for sleeping so much was always a thick dream. Colorful and filled with wishes. In the dark of the late morning with the shades pulled closed, she remembered balloons that flew up, released like doves, gently tapping each other with that balloon sound that somehow spelled her name.

She dreamt she was alone on a highway, falling into a ditch where animals bit her. Animals as deformed as ingrown toenails. There was a small pink horse that reached for her through a thicket on the side of a road. It licked her fingers with a cat's rough tongue and held her there with a hoof.

The dream reminded her of when Abby was little and she and Jeffrey took her to a fair. There were small rides and games to play; she sat on a hill and watched Jeffrey and Abby below.

At the top of the hill was a Boy Scout troop selling pumpkin donuts. Livia bought four of them, while Jeffrey and Abby went on the Ferris wheel.

Livia walked halfway down the hill. She was cold. She ate her donuts ravenously. She ate them all, out of sight from her family, and watched a dwarf pony that she heard the owner—a woman—say she kept in her house like a dog.

Other people's children rolled down the hill next to her, and she watched them, licking her fingers. The just-mowed grass stuck to the back of the children's clothes. She heard "Mom" and turned where Abby and Jeffrey were motioning for her from the donut booth. She had not seen them walk up and hoped they had not seen her.

Livia walked over to Abby, who was holding two donuts.

"Here, Mom," she said, giving her one.

"Wow," said Livia, taking it from her, the taste of sugar still in her mouth, "doesn't this look good."

Livia knows it is wrong to be so tired; she knows it is wrong to eat so much. Now that the chips are almost gone, she pours the crumbs into the onion dip container and mixes them up with a plastic spoon, then eats the stuff like stew. She looks over at the storage bins in the open closet and tries to remember if she still has those soft chocolate chip cookies. She pictures herself getting up and eating them, then picking up the clothes on the floor like Jeffrey had asked her to, putting her laundry in the basket.

She pictures herself getting back into bed and setting her alarm clock. Going back to sleep. She uses her fingers to get the last of the dip, puts the can and the chips in a black plastic bag, and ties it up. She rolls up the sheet and puts it in the laundry for Jorgen.

Livia gets up and looks at the spot where she was sitting. There is no mark from her. She is by herself, no witnesses, silent and chewing with her dreams. She keeps them to herself and stews in them alone. She gets back in bed and opens her laptop, then types her dreams in a Word document while they are fresh in her head.

Deformed horses trying to get me. Using their gross paws or hooves on the side of the road. There were also balloons that said something. Green thickets, hard to get away from the deformed animals. Thick toenails/hooves.

She does not even share her dreams with Jeffrey; not the way she had imagined she would when she was younger. When she was young, she pictured herself telling her future husband everything. She figured it would be like when she had had boyfriends before she met Jeffrey, when she was always crying, telling them her dreams in the morning, telling them how anxious she was.

She felt these sadnesses were a part of men knowing her, even if it was only a short relationship, one she ended up making shorter by saying all these things.

"I'm always a little sad," she said to the boys before Jeffrey.

She had heard that in a movie. The girl who said it was beautiful and looked good when she cried; Livia was too old to say it when she did.

Jeffrey had made it clear that he did not love these things about her. When he met her, she had been in a good place. She had been on an upswing, recently finishing college, moving to New York. For the first time in a long time she did not feel like there were tears behind her eyes.

The morning after the first night Livia and Jeffrey slept together, she told him her dream and then asked him his.

They were in her first apartment. She had had to clear a pathway to get from the bedroom door to the bed the night before: her clothes were everywhere.

"I don't remember," he said.

"Do you ever remember?" she asked.

"No," Jeffrey said. "Listening to dreams is boring."

This had never occurred to Livia before: her own dreams were so fascinating. But when she thought about listening to people who were not her lovers tell their dreams, she could see how he might be right. Still, listening to lovers' dreams was something else. She figured if she heard their dreams she would be able to understand them more deeply, and she would be able to tell how they felt about her, and if they were beginning to fall in love.

That night, before they slept together, drunk and on her bed, she had made Jeffrey take his pointer finger and pretend that finger was a person in therapy and her finger was the therapist. She told him to have a funny voice.

She had learned this in college. She had taken psychology. Children would hide behind dolls, making the dolls say what the children really felt. This was the only way to get a man to know himself: you had to sneak it out of him.

That night, Jeffrey had played along. She knew she had to get all of this out of him before they fucked. Boys would do anything to get into bed.

Livia presses "save" and puts her laptop back down on the floor. Her stomach does not feel completely full. This is part of the problem: she hates to feel empty. She wonders if there is anything else she can stuff in.

Livia looks at the print that she inherited from her parents on the wall across from the bed, thinking of what to do next. It is calming to look at the print in its too-big, black lacquer frame, outlined by glass so that the print seems to float in the middle of the wall.

It is a showpiece: the print is of a naked man with his hands held out toward the viewer, holding a globe of the earth. If she looks at it a long time, the perspective changes. The man's eyes look up, his body is bent back, and she can never decide if he is giving up the world, or taking it away.

The black lacquer of the frame does not go with what the man is doing. She has known this since she first saw the picture framed.

It had been a quick black lacquer phase, started by a side table she found at Maddy's. It was when they first moved and she had taken on their house as a project. She began on her own interiors, experimenting. Recently she told Maddy at the antique store that she is interested in doing other homes. She even got a card made:

Livia Gray Schecter
Decorator
Helping You Feel at Home

The whole thing is still new; for two years she was going to classes to get her master's in literature, but her courses ended in the spring. All summer and now fall, she cannot get herself to finish her thesis.

At the beginning of the summer she rented an office in town in order to concentrate, but ended up sleeping on the couch she had secretly bought at Ikea, or going on the Internet, or driving to the 7-Eleven for candy and chips. She will finish her thesis—she knows she will. In the meantime, until she is ready, she is using her creativity. Either that or do nothing, she told Jeffrey when she first brought home her new business cards.

Livia gets up (it is almost three) and decides to shower. She is done with the food for now.

The dread of the shower is part of the reason she stays in bed. She hates to bathe, hates being in there alone. That, and the rest of the day, waiting outside for her like an early blind date.

She quickly washes herself, doing her regular routine (armpit, armpit, crotch, ass). She ignores her body, trying to get out of the shower as fast as she can. She does not like her body anymore, not like she once did, even though she knows she is lucky: she is not as fat as she should be. She is blessed with a high metabolism; if she ate like a normal person, she is sure she would be thin.

But she does not eat like a normal person. So she has a butt that dimples and the same two-tiered hips that her mother had, a belly that slopes up from below, the beginnings of saggy breasts.

When she was younger, she loved her breasts. In her twenties, she once showed a boy her breasts in a bathroom at a party. He acted like a breast connoisseur, examining them, putting his finger below one and then the other, then nodding, as if she'd passed some test.

"Those are going to last you a long time," he said.

And he was right. They had lasted her for years. Even now, with the right bra, she can make them resemble her pre-Abby breasts. But it's not the same.

Livia steps out of the shower and dries herself (armpit, armpit, crotch, ass). She throws the wet towel in the laundry basket for Jorgen to wash.

She changes into black pants, high-heeled boots, and an off-white silk shirt, and looks at herself in the mirror, pushing back her long black hair. She smiles, then frowns, then pats the side of her pants, turns sideways, and smoothes down her stomach.

Livia tiptoes on the kitchen tile on her way out so that Jorgen will not come talk to her. The problem with Jorgen is that he is always there, knowing she sleeps late, waiting all day for her to leave her bedroom. He is always around when she just wants to eat.

Still, she doesn't want to do the laundry and Jorgen is there to do it; she hates to cook and that is Jorgen's job. Sometimes she wishes she could pay him just to come out of the basement and upstairs at certain times of the day. She could make him a schedule; she would pay him more just to stay in his room.

She lets her boots click on the patio once she is outside the threat of Jorgen asking her something. She drives into town and parks outside Maddy's.

"Why hello!" Maddy says as she walks into the store, as if she is surprised to see her. Livia goes to Maddy's at least once a week.

"Hello darling," Livia says, as if she is a little British.

Maddy is dressed in one of her usual big colorful tent dresses that always have some shade of red in them to match her bright dyed hair. Livia suspects she is sixty or so, and she seems like a mother. She waves Livia over with her ringless hand (Livia suspects a dead husband) to where she is standing by the counter with a gray-haired woman. Livia notes the antique metal business card holder with her cards in it that Maddy enthusiastically put out when Livia told her her plans.

"I'm so glad you're here!" Maddy says too loudly (Livia suspects she's a bit deaf), taking Livia's hand with her dry fingers and pulling her in.

"Livia, this is Simone. Simone, Livia. This is the woman I was telling you about!" she tells the gray-haired woman.

The woman does not look like a Simone. "Simone" is a Puerto Rican teenager—a pregnant Puerto Rican teenager—or else a Broadway actress who has a bit part in *The Lion King*. This Simone wears a multicolored scarf around her neck held by a circular silver pin.

Livia shakes Simone's hand firmly and looks into her eyes. She has a young face and her gray hair is distracting. Livia wonders how the choice was made not to dye it.

"Simone is looking for a decorator!" Maddy says, then turns to Livia and tells her that Simone has just moved to the area from Manhattan. "She's a psychiatrist," Maddy says, almost whispering.

Livia smiles, and the woman smiles back. She has very few smile lines. Perhaps the gray hair makes her look younger.

"How wonderful!" Livia says. She wants to tell Simone about her own interest in psychology, in dreams, but stops herself. Livia does not see any makeup traces on Simone's face. Perhaps Simone is just good at putting foundation on. It makes Livia uncomfortable, embarrassed that she is wearing red lipstick, makeup you can see.

"Simone says she has a great big old empty house," Maddy says.

Simone blushes. "My partner and I just moved out on the Neck, past the beach. It's an old, beautiful house, but we need help," she says.

"Maybe you should go see it, Livia," Maddy says.

"Yes, actually, do you have time now? I'm sure you're busy . . ." Simone says.

It is quick, sudden, and Livia wishes she had something she had to do, even though she wants to see the place. She thinks about taking out her Filofax "just to make sure" but stops herself. Instead she says she has some time now, she would love to see the place.

"Oh great!" Simone says.

Livia can't imagine inviting someone to her own house on a whim like that. She must seem different than she is to Simone. She tries to see outside herself. She is pretty, tall, not heavy. Perhaps she seems professional.

Maddy walks the women to the door, as if she were a mother saying goodbye to her children.

"Bye girls," Maddy says, smiling and waving to them as they each get into their cars, coincidentally parked directly behind each other, as if they had planned it perfectly, Simone's in front.

In the car, following each turn signal from Simone's navy blue Volvo, Livia thinks about Simone's "partner." Partner means lesbian or else it means a man and woman who aren't married. Livia figures that in this case it means lesbian—why else would she keep her hair gray? She follows Simone out of town and onto the long country road that leads out to the water.

Livia wonders how lesbians like to decorate. Livia's only lesbian experience was in college when a girl from her high school came to visit. She had not known her well, but the girl stayed with her in her bed. After they turned off the lights, after drinking wine, the girl told her that she had always thought Livia was pretty in high school. Then she took her hand and leaned over and kissed her.

At first Livia had kissed her back. It was a soft kiss, stubble-less, nice in a relaxing way. When the girl put her hand on her stomach, Livia let her. She let her touch her breasts, gently, making circles on her nipple.

Livia let the girl touch her over her underwear. It felt good. But when she went to go underneath it, Livia turned over and took the girl's hand away. The next day the girl left before Livia woke up.

Livia drives over the Causeway, a two-lane road with the Long Island Sound on one side and a marsh on the other, which takes you from one island—Long Island—to another part of the same island, an island within an island: Lloyd Neck. The Neck has a Nature Conservancy that was a former estate. It is where Livia pictures *The Great Gatsby* taking place. She likes this part of Long Island, although it is hard to describe to people not from here, people from back home in Philadelphia. This part of Long Island is the beautiful part, the North Shore, the old money. They are some of the only Jews there, she told her family when they first moved here four years ago, hardly believing it herself.

In winter, sometimes the Causeway freezes and the people on the Neck are stuck with themselves—they cannot get into town. The idea of this is terrible to Livia. Still, it is the most expensive place to live in the area. It is on the water.

Today the water on the Sound side is choppy. The marsh looks the same as it always does: green and boggy and dark.

Simone puts her left turn signal on not too long after they cross the Causeway, and Livia follows her onto a long paved road and then a pebbled driveway. Up ahead is a huge old white house with blue shutters. Beyond it she can see the water. Livia is excited—a house like this could be beautiful. If she is given free rein, she could go modern inside, or, if more to their taste, keep it within the time period.

She could go stark and white if they don't have children; she could do zebra and even add a hint of red.

Livia is excited, getting out of the car and following Simone to the front door.

There are so many ways she can go.

4.

Abby and Jenna sit in the lunchroom, together, alone.

"Your lawn rocks," Jenna says, out of nowhere.

Abby had not been thinking of her lawn. She turns away from the windows where she had been looking out on the shitty gray day. The windows are patterned with black stickers of seagulls so that birds do not fly into the glass and die.

"Thanks," Abby says. She had not known the lawn was something so special. She had not thought about her lawn since her father stopped asking her to mow it. Abby's lawn is in full view from the big road that goes to their school, but no one has talked about it before, not to her.

Abby is hungry but she only has a cheese sandwich with fake cheese that Jorgen made. She also has an apple. She eats half the sandwich, then folds it up in a napkin. Nothing Jorgen makes ever tastes good.

Jenna says Abby's lawn is cool, not like hers, which is not big enough.

Abby looks out the windows of the lunchroom, past the seagulls so they become blurry and hardly there, to the playing fields. She touches the smooth skin above her lip.

"You know, we should totally have some guys over to your place. We can hang out on the lawn. I'll just

35

sneak out," Jenna says, her slink of gold bracelets hitting the table.

"OK," Abby says.

Jenna says she will invite Chess Johnson, the new boy who suddenly appeared on the first day of school, already popular, as if he was just made that way and the other popular people smelled it on him. Part of it is that he is a football player and beautiful, and part of it is that he's from the city. He dates Heather Anderson, but Jenna told Abby she's fucked him two times, too. It doesn't bother Jenna that he has a girlfriend. He has a big dick, she says.

"He's cool, really," Jenna says. "I'll have him bring a friend."

Abby walks away from Jenna when the bell rings, imagining Chess Johnson on her lawn, his football thighs (she pictures him in his uniform) flattening her father's grass. His big dick, making a shadow.

Alec Sims slams Abby's locker from behind her, just as she is opening up her backpack. At least once a day this happens: Alec's big freckled hand surprises her. Alec's locker is next to hers but she does not slam his, even when he is turned around, high-fiving boys' hands. It is as if he closes her locker as a reflex, leaving her locked out, holding her things, frazzled. She hates him.

"Monkey," he says.

She looks up at him, into his small blue eyes and freckled face, and watches his smile straighten. Accidentally, Abby reaches her hand up to touch her lip.

"What did you do? Shave?" he asks. His face looks serious.

Abby looks up at him, his red hair almost pink, falling down over his eyes like all the boys. She is still squatting—she had been trying to find a book.

"Fucker," she says, raising her new eyebrows on purpose.

"*Fucker*," he mimics in a high, whiney voice. "Hair grows back."

Alec has a big ass and a round face. He seemed popular last year, but this year he is shorter and fatter, less cool. Still, he is on the lacrosse team and she's seen him hanging out with Chess Johnson. She worries if Jenna asks Chess he will bring Alec to her lawn.

She looks up at him again, but he is walking away, not even looking back to see her expression. She decides not to open her locker again. She decides to skip Tech class. She has been working on a decoy duck, which she has no use for. It was that or a lamp base, and for some reason the duck seemed like a better idea.

But now that she has seen how ugly it is, and how it doesn't look like a duck, really, and how she will probably just throw it out once she is finished; she wishes she had gone with the lamp base.

Abby decides to head to the red doors to smoke. Her duck can wait.

She walks down the hall and hopes none of the mean boys are out there. There is the excitement, always, of a smoke, of being in the chilled air, of a break.

But then the other part: opening the door just a bit and seeing their jeans low on their waists, wearing puffy vests, smoking their cigarettes with their two fingers, the boy way. They ignore her, or worse, say her name funny, make fun of her hair.

Abby opens the door, feels the wind, and sees an arm with a blue parka. She thinks about closing the door, sucking it up and going back to her duck, but it is too late, the bell rings. She slips out the door and sees Chess Johnson, alone, smoking the girl way.

"Hey," he says. Chess Johnson is hot: brown hair covering one eye so he has to flip his head back to see, brown eyes and a turned up nose.

She half smiles, relieved.

Just this morning, in French class, Jenna had thrown Abby a note that she read while trying to look like she was paying attention to the teacher.

Look at Chess Johnson's boner! it said.

Abby scanned her way past the other desks, slowly, to the right, where Chess's lap was a pitched-jean tent. It looked big, hitting the bottom of his desk. He was leaning over it, writing in his notebook.

Abby drew Chess Johnson, naked, leaning over, his huge penis lifting up the desk, and threw it back to Jenna when the teacher turned to the blackboard.

Jenna wrote back: *I'm going to pee in my pants!!!*

"Hi," she says to Chess, leaning against the brick and taking her cigarettes from the inside pocket of her army coat, then lighting up.

"Jenna says you have a killer lawn," he says. Abby glances down at his fly: flat.

Abby looks back up at his face. One of his front teeth is chipped a little. His lips are chapped and have small dark red crevices in them. Before this moment, before he knew about her lawn, she had never seen him up close.

"It's OK," Abby says, trying not to sound too proud.

"Jenna said maybe we can all hang there tonight," he says, flicking his neck back. Jenna showed her a hickey he had given her on her stomach, low, like a secret tattoo.

The door opens a bit and Abby and Chess both quickly flick their cigarettes.

A hand reaches outside the door and Abby sees Jenna's gold bangles.

"Boo!" Jenna says, poking her face, and then her body, out. "Scared you!" she laughs.

Abby laughs too.

"I was just talking about you," Chess says, leaning over to pick up his still-smoking cigarette.

"Yeah?" Jenna says, lighting a cigarette.

"Yeah. We were talking about Abby's house."

"Oh, yeah," Jenna says. "We should all go over tonight. Me and Abby can go to my house first and steal some beer from my mom."

Abby knows that Jenna gets a ride home from a different boy almost every day, but today she takes the bus with Abby. They sit in the way-way-back: buses are for losers.

Abby picks at the sticky tape that covers up the tears in the seat in front of them, all gummy in her hands, and tells Jenna about what Alec said about her moustache.

"What's important," Jenna says, "is that he noticed."

Abby looks at Jenna's smile and copies it. Perhaps Jenna is right. Already things are coming true: tonight she will have boys on her lawn.

The bus drops them outside an olive-green ranch house perched on a small hill. They walk up the sloped driveway and Jenna takes a Hello Kitty keychain from her pocketbook.

"No one's home," Jenna says, opening the door.

The house is lightless. Once in, it seems as if it's night outside.

"My room's down there," she says, pointing down a long dark hall to their right. "And my grandparents' room is down there," she says, pointing down another long hall in the opposite direction.

The house has a smell that Abby cannot identify. She begins to put down her book bag by the front door but Jenna picks it up and gives it back to her.

"My mom and stepdad live down here," she says, walking toward another door and opening it.

Abby follows Jenna down the stairs to the basement. There is a beaded curtain that hangs down at the bottom that Jenna parts to reveal a tiny apartment. It has all the things a house would have, but in one big room. There is a maroon tapestry draped from the ceiling that hides part of the bed; there is a whole kitchen space, and another space made up of two black leather couches and a TV. It looks like someone is playing house.

Jenna gets them both Cokes from the fridge, then reaches up and opens one of the food cabinets. It is stacked with cans: rows and rows of Bud Light. Jenna grabs an armful and hands some down to Abby. Abby opens her backpack and puts them in, then looks up again at the edge of the "bedroom" where the tapestry is.

"They're married," Jenna says, like she can tell what Abby is thinking. She gives her more beer, then fills up her own backpack. Abby watches as Jenna walks behind the stairs into the darker part of the basement and comes back with a bunch of cans to re-stock the cabinet.

Abby follows Jenna up the stairs and down the long dark hall to her room, which is painted pink but covered with posters. There is a poster of a unicorn that looks like she forgot to take it down after junior high, a black-and-white one of a man and a woman kissing in France, some posters of hip-hop stars, and a couple of shiny ads of boys ripped from magazines.

Jenna turns on a small light on her night table.

"Those were my mom's," she says, pointing to a bunch of bookshelves filled with old dolls. "Some of them are worth a lot."

Abby looks over at the shelves. There is a doll for each country, each one dressed in its native clothing. The American one wears a cowboy outfit and Abby wonders if that is how people who are not American imagine people here. Jorgen must have pictured her family that way—she wonders if he was disappointed when they were not waiting at the airplane gate in

41

braids and cowhide. She looks for the Swedish doll and finds it: blonde with braids and a long blue dress, carrying some kind of jug.

The dolls look dusty and sad.

Jenna opens the window and the two girls stick their heads out and light cigarettes. Jenna shows Abby how she fluffs up the hedge outside the window after each time she sneaks out. Abby wonders if Jenna's mom and stepdad can hear her above them when she walks around. Her own parents might hear her sometimes too. Once her father told her he'd heard her exercising, even though she had not been.

In her own house, Abby's bedroom is directly above her parents, who are on the first floor. Below her parents, in the basement, is Jorgen. All stacked on top of each other.

Abby's and Jenna's elbows touch on the sill, both of them trying to fit their top halves out the window. They take drags at the same time and bump arms and laugh.

"My real dad lives in New Jersey," Jenna says. "He comes to get me on his motorcycle every third Saturday."

"He motorcycles all the way from there?" Abby asks.

"Yeah. He went to our high school too, but he dropped out. He smokes pot. My mom hates him."

It is weird to hear Jenna say things like this. It is weird to hear her say anything that someone could make fun of.

She wishes she could tell Jenna something back. Abby inhales, blushes, and says it: "I'm a virgin."

Jenna coughs and laughs, and Abby immediately regrets saying anything.

"What?" Jenna says. "Everyone knows that!"

"We should totally get fucked up for Pep Rally," Jenna says.

They are on Abby's lawn at night with Chess and Alec. Abby looks up at the sky. Full moon. She is not cold at all.

Abby has only said "Hi" to Alec since he got there, stepping out of Chess's car parked across the road. For a quick moment the streetlights made it look like the boy getting out of the back seat was blond, not red-headed, and for a second Abby was excited and relieved. Then Alec walked around the car behind Jenna and Chess, his fat ass following him.

Alec and Abby have been ignoring each other while Jenna does most of the talking and Chess laughs with her. Sometimes Alec says something to Chess—some inside boy joke—but otherwise Alec is quiet too and Abby is relieved. So far, nothing about her hair.

Abby goes for another beer, tossing the can she is done with toward the woods like the boys did.

"Whoa there!" Chess says, looking at her. "You're thirsty, huh?"

She looks down at her beer, confused. She thought she had been drinking the same amount as everyone else. She stops and feels different—it is different than anything a boy has said to her: "Whoa there." *Whoa there.* Saying "You're"—it's like he's a dad. A little. She looks at him dead on, and they all laugh. Abby blushes but not the way she usually does. Her cheeks are warm already so she hardly feels it.

She pushes the hood of her sweatshirt off her head.

"I'm feeling it," Jenna says, lighting a cigarette and lying back on the grass, straightening her legs out. "The stars are totally cool."

Abby lies down next to her and so does Chess. Then Alec falls back. Abby looks at the sky and thinks of pointing out the constellations. When she was little her father would take her to the planetarium. The only thing she could ever remember was Orion's Belt, but she liked being in the dark there, all those stars around you, but also like you were trapped in the sky. Like the sky was like the real sky, going down to the horizon, but also keeping you inside in a way you didn't feel like with the real sky—like you were trapped in the world. Her first step outside the planetarium was always a relief. But then she always looked forward to the next time when she could feel that way: covered in stars.

She wants to ask them if they can see Orion, take someone's finger in her hand when they tell her they don't. She wants to point with their finger in hers: *There*.

Abby feels good. She watches as Chess reaches for Jenna's hand in the grass, then watches as they both get up, as if his hand has spoken to hers, as if it is a secret signal, and begin to walk away toward the woods, pushing against each other playfully. She wonders how far they will walk until they stop.

Abby stands up too. She takes a drag from her cigarette. She is drunk but she remembers to look up at the house. All of the upstairs windows are dark, but the tiny basement window is lit with Jorgen's fluorescent tube lights, as usual. She wonders how he can sleep like that, if he is always just a little awake.

Suddenly Abby feels herself being pushed forward, her hands hitting the grass, her cigarette flying away.

"Ow!" she says, and feels herself being turned over. She is drunk, and Alec is on top of her, his bangs sweeping her forehead.

Alec begins to kiss her and Abby opens her eyes because it does not seem real. Abby has kissed boys two times before: once at Truth or Dare before they moved, in sixth grade, and once, for a longer time, on their trip to a resort in Jamaica last year with a boy from Maine. His kisses were hard, deep: it felt like his tongue was searching for something inside her. Abby thought the boy might be doing it wrong.

Alec's kisses feel like a warm, wet washcloth. He is soft—too soft: she puts her tongue farther into his mouth, trying to make him kiss harder.

It feels strange, like he is trying to be gentle.

"Tell me when to stop," he says, and lifts up her shirt.

She looks down at him: all his touches feel like he is testing a hot light bulb with his fingertips. He sucks her breasts lightly, like a baby. She touches the top of his head. He goes for the button on her jeans and she tells him: stop.

Later, in her room, after the boys have driven away quietly, Abby pulls up her shirt and looks at her nipples in her bathroom mirror. They are swollen; there is a hickey on her breast. She remembers how light

Alec's mouth had felt, and thinks about how touching the same place for a long time, hard or not, will always leave a mark.

5.

The kitchen is too small, so they eat in the dining room. They each have their seats: Livia and Jeffrey at the heads of the table, Abby and Jorgen opposite each other in the middle.

Livia has been waiting until now to tell them.

"I got my first client today," she says.

"Wow," Jeffrey says, sounding completely un-wowed, eating his fish, not looking up.

"I didn't know you were still doing that," Abby says.

"Of course, honey," Livia says, annoyed. What does her daughter think she does all day?

Livia picks out the carrots in her salad. She hates carrots unless they are scooping up onion dip. She is not hungry: on her way home from Simone's she stopped for pizza and ate four slices in the car.

"It's a really big deal," Livia says. "It's this amazing old house on the Neck."

"Wow," Jeffrey says again in the same voice. "Sounds like you have your work cut out for you."

Livia looks over at Jeffrey, at the top of his head. He is good-looking, but was never her type, which is strange. Women always say what a handsome man her husband is: his thick head of curly hair, olive skin that tans him exotic in the summer. He is sturdy-looking, strong.

For a long time she liked blond, young-looking men. But when, some years ago, Livia went to Dr. Courtenay (an older man) for therapy, she talked for a while about how she craved a black man; how sometimes, if she thought about it too much, her mind planned all kinds of ways she could try to get one.

"Have you encountered many African Americans in your life?" the doctor asked.

Dr. Courtenay was almost completely bald and smoked a pipe like he thought he was Freud. This made the basement of his house where he had his office smell like Livia's grandfather. When she left she always smelled like him.

When Livia and her brother were small they had a black nanny who died in their house. Rich had found her, hardly breathing on the kitchen floor, and called out to Livia who was playing in the other room.

Livia was six and Rich was four. They sat beside the big dead body until their parents got home. Livia remembered touching the ruffles of her apron. Rich had cried.

Livia figured her mother would take care of them after that, so she was not sad like her brother. She was glad the nanny was no longer making noises.

Only she was wrong: another black nanny came to take care of them only a few days later. Rich cried again (he was always weaker than Livia, and still is) but Livia ignored her. She was mad at her mother, she learned in therapy, but took it out on the nanny.

Livia stayed in therapy for two years, waiting to be happy. Dr. Courtenay put her on antidepressants, which helped. She told him her dreams—she printed them out before each visit and read them to him.

But after awhile she began to sleep through the appointments. She stopped answering his calls. It was exhausting, blaming her mother for everything.

At the dining room table Livia tells her family and Jorgen about how her new client, Simone, is a psychiatrist. She tells them how she was there just this afternoon to see the layout of the house.

"That's great," Jorgen says.

"She just moved here," Livia says.

Livia felt so good during the day, going into Simone's house and looking all around. She had followed Simone into the foyer of the house and watched as she took off her shoes.

"Would you mind taking yours off too?" Simone asked, pushing her gray hair behind her ear while pulling her flats off.

Livia looked down at Simone's bare feet.

"Oh, of course," she said. "I do the same in my house."

This was a lie. Livia does not do this. There is a certain type of person who does this; Livia thinks it is controlling.

She took off her shoes and put them together by the door. She peeked into the next room (the living room?). The house was not unpacked; there were boxes everywhere.

"Can I use the bathroom?" Livia asked.

"Sure, but do you mind using the one in the bedroom? I still don't have toilet paper and soap downstairs . . ." Simone said.

"That's fine," Livia said, glad she would get a peek.

She followed Simone upstairs, the Berber carpeting rough beneath her feet. They would need to take that out.

The bed in Simone's bedroom was unmade, and clothes were thrown on the floor. There were more boxes, unpacked and unlabeled, piled against the wall.

"Excuse our mess," Simone said, sounding embarrassed.

Livia looked on the floor. Women's clothes: a dress, a T-shirt, a pair of jeans. One pair of white panties with no stains on them, their crotch facing up as if someone had just stepped out of them.

"Oh please," Livia said. "You should see my place."

This was another lie—her place is clean. She has Jorgen.

Simone still had not said her partner's name. Livia looked at the bureau: hard, dark wood with a jewelry box and perfume. So far, no man.

Simone directed her to the bathroom. Inside it was stark white with a clear shower curtain.

Livia turned on the water, pretending to pee, and looked in the shower. Lined on the edge of the tub were good-smelling, special soaps, and expensive shampoos and conditioners. There was an all-in-one shampoo/conditioner for dyed hair.

Above the sink, in the mirrored cabinet, were ladies' pink razors and Motrin. There was also a prescription for Paxil.

"Gail M. Philips," it said.

"It's a girl!" Livia thought. She closed the cabinet and smiled at herself in the mirror, strangely satisfied, as if she had just eaten.

She knew what to look for now. Suddenly everything in Simone's house looked like it belonged to a lesbian: the underwear, the white terry cloth robe on the back of the door, the soap and toothbrush . . .

"Where would you like to start?" Livia asked, coming out of the bathroom and turning off the light.

Livia followed Simone downstairs. The house was in good shape, Livia thought, feeling the smooth railing. Everything looked like it was the highest quality; it felt clean.

If it had been up to Livia, her house would be this way too. But Jeffrey always says she doesn't understand money, so he is mostly in charge of it, and he is cheap.

The furniture they have is good, but when Livia went with Jeffrey to buy it he always went for the lowest-priced line. When Livia began to go shopping alone he came at her with the credit card statements, hounding her about each purchase.

Still, it is worth withstanding his yelling to have nice things. But his cheapness is something Livia hates about Jeffrey. She hates it more when she sees the way other people live. With other people's money, she thinks, with Simone's money, she could spend as if she did not have a husband. Simone does not have a husband, and she likes to spend.

Livia's mother-in-law is cheap too. That's where Jeffrey gets it from. Headie keeps coffee that is left over in the pot and re-heats it in a pan the next day; she keeps the house freezing so that the heating bills are low; she freezes everything that you give her fresh, and takes out the frozen things for you to eat. Livia hardly eats when they visit her, running errands and then zipping over to Dunkin Donuts, eating in the car.

"Have a seat," Simone said, pointing to a white couch in the living room. Livia sat while Simone walked into the kitchen. Simone had nice hips, a small but round butt, and good shoulders. Livia liked the way she looked from the back.

"Do you want some wine?" Simone asked.

Livia wanted some wine very badly. Sitting in the living room, the big windows looking out at the ocean, Livia could not think of anything better.

"That would be great," Livia said, and Simone came back in with two full glasses of red.

"Cheers," Simone said, leaning over just as Livia was putting the glass to her mouth. The evening light was coming in beautifully, and the glasses caught it and shined.

"Oh, cheers," Livia said, clinking back. She watched Simone sit down across from her in a matching white chair and bring the glass to her lips. She watched her smell the wine, swirl it, and take a small sip.

"I read about this," Simone said, nodding toward the wine. "It's supposed to have a great bouquet."

Livia had never understood wine tasting. She still didn't understand what people meant by "dry." She could never taste the cherryness, the smokiness, the butteriness. She nodded at Simone.

"Yes, very smooth," she said, taking a small sip too.

"So," Simone said, leaning forward, "how long have you been a decorator?"

Livia began to talk about her own home renovations as if they'd been for other people, embellishing things here and there. She told her how she was finishing her thesis and how she has been working as a decorator in the meantime. She has a passion for it, she told Simone, and she studied art.

"Sometimes I wish I had studied art," Simone said, putting her feet to the side and curling her legs up under her. Her toenails were painted—surprisingly—red.

"Me too," Livia said, then realized what she had said. "I mean, I wish I had gotten my master's in it."

"Still," Simone said, "it sounds like you have a lot of creative outlets."

"Oh, yes," Livia said. "I love what I do."

"So," Livia says at dinner, "if I make a bunch of money from this, I think we should get a pool in the backyard."

"Awesome," Abby says.

"Yeah, well, let's see how it goes," Jeffrey says.

Jorgen looks up from the fish and smiles.

"I don't know why you say that, Jeffrey. I might be able to afford it myself."

"OK," Jeffrey says in his calm voice. "Let's see how it goes."

Sometimes Livia is sure she hates him. She is sure he is the reason she eats and sleeps too much. She remembers when she was younger, all the energy she had, staying up forever, living on coffee. Food had not been an issue then. She was happy to get naked in front of anyone.

She had been that way with Jeffrey in the beginning too. He had made her feel sexy. He told her he wished he could take a picture of her ass. Once, in the beginning, while making love, he told her, "This is all yours, you have all of me."

When they have sex now it is mostly from behind. She doesn't like to kiss him, even though he likes it. She always sees him looking at her lips when she is facing him. She didn't know what anyone meant when they talked about having bad sex until two years into her marriage when it became clear.

Still, she had loved him. He had loved her. He had wanted a baby and she had said OK.

"Well, so far it's going great," Livia says, moving her salad to the other side of her plate. "She's a great woman, and a lesbian."

"Really?" Abby says.

Livia nods.

"What is lez-bian?" Jorgen asks.

Abby laughs.

"It is when a woman loves another woman," Jeffrey says softly.

Jorgen blushes.

"Oh yes," he says.

"I haven't met her partner yet. I'm sure she's nice, though," Livia says.

Jeffrey nods.

Livia never told Jeffrey about her lesbian experience in college. Not that she was embarrassed. Not really. She just figured he wouldn't like it: he never wanted to hear about her old boyfriends, or men she had had sex with. When they were first together and she told him those things, he would cringe. Still, she kept going, watching his face as she told each story. She wanted him to tell her if he didn't want her to tell him. It bothered her that he just fiddled with things while she talked, tried to change the subject.

She went on with the stories, until finally, one day when she was telling him about a married movie producer she'd met in a New York nightclub, he said it: stop.

Livia loved to hear about Jeffrey's old exploits. He didn't have nearly as many as she did. He had had a few girlfriends and lost his virginity to his high school sweetheart. And there was the Mexican girl he met on spring break.

Livia loved the story of the Mexican girl. She loved to hear how he and his friends met her in a bar with her friends while he was on some kind of "guys" vacation in college, and how she spoke little English.

She wore a bikini top, he said, and a sarong bottom. She had long black hair. She wanted him to fuck her in the ass so he did.

"May I be excused from the table?" Abby asks.

Livia can see Abby has only eaten half of her fish, but she doesn't say anything.

"Yes, you may," Livia says, just like her mother used to.

On her second glass of wine, Livia asked Simone what her partner's name was.

"Gail," Simone said.

"Have you been together for a long time?" Livia asked.

"Going on eleven years," Simone said, lifting her glass.

"My husband and I have been together for twenty," Livia said. "We have a fifteen-year-old daughter."

"Oh, Gail has a son. He used to spend part of the time with us and part with his father," Simone said, "but now he's living with us full-time. He plays football." Simone rolled her eyes.

Livia smiled. She took a sip of wine and told Simone how she thought Abby had her art genes.

"And your husband?" Simone asked.

"He's not creative," Livia said.

"No, I mean, what does he do?" she asked.

"He's a lawyer. Real estate. I know nothing about it."

"Tell me about it," Simone said. "Gail is a lawyer too. I never know what she's working on, and she doesn't like to talk about it either. We moved here because she couldn't take the city anymore. We both have to commute because my practice is there too, but that's fine."

Livia wondered for a second if Jeffrey wanted to talk to her about his work but didn't. She was feeling good from the wine and did not want to think about Jeffrey.

Livia looked at Simone. She had nice white teeth. Livia tried to picture what she looked like when she was younger, with darker hair. She wondered if she'd ever loved a man.

"I'm going to use the bathroom," Livia said, setting her glass on the table. She reached down to get her purse and knocked the red wine over onto the white couch.

"Oh my God!" Livia said, seeing the red spill and spread. She ran to the kitchen, took a roll of paper towels off the counter, wet them in the sink, and brought them back.

"I'm so sorry!" Livia said on her knees, scrubbing the stain on the couch.

"Oh, don't worry," Simone said. "We're getting new furniture, remember?"

She put her arm on Livia's, then gently flipped the cushion the wine had spilled on.

"See?" Simone said, "No big deal."

Livia stared at the suddenly-white-again couch. She got off her knees and looked at Simone smiling, the stain no longer visible. Amazing the way Simone had done that. How easy things seemed.

"You're right," Livia said, taking a deep breath, relieved. "Wait until you see the ideas I have for this place."

Livia decided not to use the bathroom. She got up and reached out her arm to Simone.

"It was so nice to talk with you a bit, but I should get going," Livia said.

"It was," Simone said. "Let's meet next week to go over some ideas."

"Fabulous!" Livia said, and Simone took her hand and kissed her cheek.

Livia blushed, turned, and left. She got in the car and drove out the driveway, down the Causeway, off the Neck. It was nice with the wine while it was still light out. She did not mind driving alone. Still, she was hungry. She headed toward town.

6.

At dusk Headie sits at the computer. It is bright and makes her happy, the light from the thing.

Millie finally left after spending the day with Headie, taking a break only for egg salad on rye, showing her how to get on the email.

Millie patiently sat while Headie wrote her first messages:

DEAR JEFFREY I AM ON THE COMPUTER LOVE MOTHER

and

DEAR ABBY I AM ON THE COMPUTER NOW LOVE BUBBE

and

DEAR LIVIA LOOK AT ME LOVE HEADIE

Now alone, Headie sits back down and presses the button Millie had shown her to press every time the screen goes black. She waits for someone to write her back.

Three hours and fifty-two minutes later, still at the table, waiting, Headie hears the sound. She clicks, like Millie said, on the tiny envelope, and up comes a note from her granddaughter.

From: abbyschecter15@yahoo.com
To: headragoldstein@aol.com

Dear Bubbe—
Dad said he got you a computer. Congrats.
I am bored. I'm supposed to be doing homework (don't tell my parents).
How is Aunt Millie? What's new at the synagogue? Are you doing any online shopping?
Love,
Abby

Headie reads the email three times. She loves that she can save the note and keep it for later. It is like frozen food.

She thanks God Livia had a girl. She remembers Livia pregnant in her flower-patterned smock. They all sat in the backyard on one of their visits, Headie and Jeffrey drinking Bloody Marys while Livia sipped a V8. Livia spotted a white rabbit in the backyard woods and the three of them decided together that it was good luck.

Livia had wanted to call the baby Anemone until Headie made Jeffrey put his foot down. Abigail was a good name, even if she was named for Headie's mother, Anna. Somebody had to be named after her, her mother had been dead so long. Abby's middle name was Anemone.

When Abby was born she came out jaundiced and ugly. Livia sat in the hospital with her yellow baby. Jeffrey sat beside her on the single bed, patting down Abby's black hair.

"Mom, come here. Meet your beautiful granddaughter," Jeffrey said.

Jeffrey had been in the room the whole time, telling Livia to breathe and push. They had done a demonstration of their breathing exercises for Headie and Allen on the floor in the living room weeks before. They both watched as Livia pretended to push and squeezed Jeffrey's hand until it was white. Everyone looked between Livia's legs where the baby was supposed to come out until Livia sighed, unclasped Jeffrey's hand, and said, "And that's it!"

When Abby got older, Livia put her hair in pigtails. She dressed her in dresses but let her play in the dirt.

When they left Abby with Headie for their first childless weekend, she made sure that the baby took two baths a day. Headie soaped up her baby skin and let her splash in the warm water. She wrapped her in her baby bathrobe, then let Abby run around with no clothes on. It was easier with a granddaughter, Headie thought. How happy she seemed.

Headie will write back in a bit, she decides. For now she unplugs her computer and plugs in her phone the way Millie showed her, then lies back down on her kitchen floor. On her back, with the phone plugged in, she listens to the sounds of the house.

She is not uncomfortable, lying on her back. Her kitchen is carpeted. That had been Allen's idea when they bought the house, and it felt just right when he said it. You never had to worry about slipping.

Headie lies on her back and remembers her own pregnancy. She had not done Lamaze. They didn't have that then. Everything she remembers about being pregnant is uncomfortable.

When she was seven and a half months pregnant, they went to a wedding for a cousin of her first husband in the Poconos. All the rooms at the recommended hotel were sold out, so they had to stay at a honeymoon lodge. In their room there was a mirror on the ceiling and the night they got there Gene looked up at it, snickered, and fell asleep.

After the wedding reception, Headie felt huge and tired. She took off her clothes and lay naked on her back on the bed. She looked up at her big belly while Gene turned on his stomach and began to snore.

Headie was tired from the wedding; she had sat, bored, at their table, eating the candies from the dish while Gene danced with one of the bridesmaids for more than one dance.

The ceremony had been a religious one, and it made Headie remember her own wedding. It was small, in her father's house in the living room. Before their witnesses and before God, Gene and Headie had promised to take care.

In the honeymoon suite Headie looked at herself on the ceiling mirror and tried to imagine what God thought now. She wondered if she looked the way her reflection did to Him, and what He thought when He saw the line that stretched up her stomach and the lightning-rod zigzags—those terrible stretch marks—on the sides of her hips. What did God think when He looked inside her husband's head and saw other women there?

What did God see when she closed her eyes and couldn't see anything? Did God see that even with Gene beside her she was still alone?

7.

The next morning, when Abby goes to her locker, she waits for Alec to say something.

Alec opens his locker gently, and she can feel the air beside her. She wonders if she likes him, really, or if it is exciting just because he likes her.

She waits for him to talk, but he gets his books, slams his locker, and walks away.

She writes Jenna in French: *Why is A not talking to me?*

Jenna writes back: *He says he never talked to you before so why would he talk to you now?*

After class she sees Jenna in the hall, smiling. Jenna runs up to her and hugs her.

"He's an ass," she says. "C'mon you ex-monkey."

They walk down the hall together. Abby loves to watch boys' eyes flit to Jenna. It means they see her too.

"Besides," Jenna says, "you should just feel bad for him. His dad got fired from his job and is going to teach Driver's Ed. And they have to quit the Club."

The Club is the Summer Club. It is a club that neither Abby's family nor Jenna's belongs to. Abby went there, once, when she first moved here, with a girl named Robin who had liked her for what seemed like a minute.

At the Summer Club they have small pieces of paper called "chits" that you use like money, writing your member number on them and ordering whatever you want at the snack bar. Everyone at the Club calls each other's parents by "Mrs." and "Mr." which is normal but sounds different for some reason—more important.

Abby tries to feel sorry for Alec. Soon his father will be the one to step on the passenger-side brake of the Driver's Ed car when she presses the gas to turn a corner.

"Look—see how she isn't hairy anymore?" Jenna says. "I plucked her."

They are outside the red doors at lunchtime. Jenna is talking about Abby to two boys in eleventh grade she doesn't know.

Jenna points at Abby.

The boys laugh, but Jenna apologizes later, when they are alone in the bathroom. She says she just talks shit like that when she is with those guys.

Abby looks at herself in the mirror, featherless, smooth. She forgives Jenna without saying a word.

"Do you think that Alec will ever talk to me?" Abby asks Jenna.

"Probably not . . . He's probably already over it," Jenna says.

Abby is surprised. She could hardly sleep all night and thought of it as soon as she woke up this morning, but she has removed Alec from it, so it is just tongue and sky.

Still, she feels angry. He makes her feel like she doesn't exist at all.

Before seventh period, in the hallway, Alec's hand reaches in front of Abby and slams her locker door like before.

"You fucking faggot!" she says, the words coming out of her suddenly. She looks up at him; his face is red and she feels scared for a second.

She watches him look at her. "You're an ugly bitch," he says back, quickly, almost whispering, then walks away. Abby watches his big butt go down the hall.

The bell rings and other kids begin to leave their classrooms. The hall gets loud and busy, but Abby stands still, holding her books, following Alec's back with her eyes. She hopes he is as sad as she is, not because of what she said, but because, like her, he wishes he hadn't said it in the first place.

8.

Livia sits on the sheet on the floor in her bedroom and eats Cheez Doodles quickly, then switches to chocolate-covered gummy bears. She goes from salty to sweet, then back again.

It is 3:07 p.m., and she has only just gotten out of bed.

She hears Jorgen drop something. Sometimes she thinks she should make up rules. Like, from eight a.m. to three p.m., Jorgen has to leave the house. Livia can go out right before Abby comes home from school, then everyone (or Jorgen, or whoever cares) will think she has been doing something all day.

The day is big, long, and there are a million years until nighttime.

When she is finished eating, Livia goes back to bed, reaches for her computer, and puts it on her lap.

Earlier she had typed her dream: *a woman (maybe Simone's Gail) on a boat eating something I cannot see. The sky is too blue, and looks scary. Trying to get her to come to shore—something is important. Don't remember what. A dog on the shore, barking at another dog on the boat.*

She reads it again, then checks her email. Spam. No fun. Then: headragoldstein@aol.com. What is she doing on the Internet?

She reads her mother-in-law's email, all caps, one line. She writes her back.

From: livia@liviathedesigner.com
To: headragoldstein@aol.com

Dear Headie-
Look at you! How did you get online? I hope you are en-joying it.
I will write more later. I'm off to the gym, and then to meet with a new decorating client.
Love,
Livia

"Did you know your mother is on the Internet?" Livia asks when Jeffrey gets home.

Livia is dressed, finally. She is clean and feels good, ready to go just as her husband is done with his day.

She yells across the hall from the bedroom into his study, where he puts his receipts and coins from his pockets and slips of paper with all the things he has written down all day. Livia has never even tried to read what the papers say. She leaves them there, then every once in a while she will see that they are gone. Papers piled up, little notes, then thrown away as if written for no reason.

"What?" he asks.

Livia stands in the doorway watching him change out of his suit and hang it in the study's closet. She doesn't like his body anymore, the way he has become hunched over, his belly larger, almost like a woman's.

When they were first together, she remembers looking at the muscles on the side of his stomach when they made love.

"Your mother is on the computer," she says. "I got an email from her."

"Oh yeah, I forgot to tell you," he says, now only in his socks, underwear, and undershirt. He opens the bureau drawer to get his jeans out. "I bought her a laptop."

Livia knows that Jeffrey has not forgotten to tell her, but has not told her on purpose. His mother will write her emails now, and she will answer them, dutifully.

"Funny," she says, walking to the TV room where Abby is watching a reality show. Three people are in a hot tub. Livia waits a minute and watches before sitting down next to her daughter.

"Did you know that Bubbe has a computer?" she asks.

Abby brushes her hair back from her face. She looks better lately, Livia has noticed. She looks at her daughter watching TV and not looking at her. That's it! Her eyebrows are plucked.

"Yeah, she wrote me," Abby says. "It's kind of funny."

"Did Daddy tell you?" Livia says.

"Yeah, he told me he was sending her a laptop," Abby says.

Livia watches as Jeffrey walks into the room, smoothing his jeans down at the pockets.

"Hi Daddy," Abby says, smiling.

RACHEL SHERMAN

"Hi hon," he says, kissing the top of her head and sitting down next to her. The three of them sit on the couch, Abby in the middle.

"Why didn't you tell me?" Livia asks. She has her eyes on the TV: two girls are kissing one boy in the hot tub.

"What?" Jeffrey says.

"About the computer! Why didn't you tell me?" Livia says.

She looks at Jeffrey and sees him sigh.

"Liv, I told you: I forgot."

"You didn't forget to tell Abby," she says, getting up and walking out of the room, slamming the door.

When they were first married, her temper would start big fights. They both slammed doors, yelled, one time Livia even spit at Jeffrey. It was terrible now that he didn't fight back. He didn't even follow her out of the room to see if she was OK. She could cry now, but he would not comfort her.

Livia turns around and looks at the door, then goes back in where Abby and Jeffrey sit, both watching TV, his arm around her, as if nothing has changed.

"I'm leaving," she says, taking her coat from the closet, getting the keys from the table, and slamming the front door.

As she walks to the car she can see her daughter and husband in the window, still sitting in the same place, still watching people kiss.

70

9.

From: jwschecter@schecterglasspeters.com
To: headragoldstein@aol.com

Hi Mother—

I'm so glad you got the computer in one piece and that Millie helped you set it up. She seems to be good with computers.

I hope you see how much your life can expand. The Internet is an amazing thing, and you can go all over the world (I know you miss traveling).

I know you weren't interested in getting a computer, but now that you have one, I hope you will take advantage of it. It will be especially nice for Abby to be able to write her Bubbe.

Love,
Jeffrey

Jeffrey W. Schecter
Attorney at Law
Schecter, Glass and Peters Associates

Headie reads her son's email at her kitchen table, then scoots off the chair and lies on the floor. She reaches her hands in the air, stretching, and looks up at her fingers, at her rings. Headie has had two lives. Two rings, two men, one bigger than the other.

When Jeffrey was little Gene worked at the bank. Headie and her son stayed home.

She had wanted a girl, and two weeks after Jeffrey was born, Headie tied a pink ribbon on the top of his head and strolled him through the neighborhood. It made her feel good when she thought that people thought she had a daughter. Women would ask her what her name was. Headie would tell them: Victoria.

At the park, she sat the baby in her lap and rocked it back and forth. She knew that Jeffrey was an ugly girl, but that was not the point. She carried on like this for weeks, until someone from the synagogue saw her and told Gene.

Gene was not mad—he was not a man with a temper—but he sat her down on the couch to explain.

Gene lifted baby Jeffrey out of his playpen.

"Look at our little boy!" he said, putting Jeffrey's face in front of his mother's. Jeffrey and his father laughed and Headie turned away and breathed. She looked in the kitchen. She would have to start cooking soon. She saw dirt in the corner tile. Then she turned back and took the baby from Gene's arms. There was nothing to say, and she knew it. It was understood.

Headie stayed home with Jeffrey. She made sure that things went smoothly for her husband. Gene was tired after work, and since she was never sure that he really loved her, she placed the scotch he liked right next to his hand on the end table, and took off his shoes while sitting on the floor.

Headie sits up. She wants to use the computer again. It is exciting, the way it waits for her on the table.

Each time she is not sure what to do next, she can just go to it.

She puts one hand on the chair, one on the table, and hoists herself up.

From: headragoldstein@aol.com
To: livia@liviathedesigner.com

TO LIVIA HOW AREYOU. I AM WELL AND LIKE THECOMPUTER. MILLIE IS FINETO. I AM GLAD YOU ARE WORKING AD BUSY. I HAVE BEEN BUSY WITH THE COMPUTER LOVE-HEADIE

Headie presses the "send" button, then writes to Abby.

From: headragoldstein@aol.com
To: abbyschecter15@yahoo.com

ABBY DO YOU LIKE THE SNOW. THEY ARE TALKINGSNOW HERE ALREADY.

DO YOU REMEMBER WHENYOU AND YOUR PARENTS GOTSTUCK UP HERE IN THE STORM IT WAS YEARS ANDYEARS AGO AND YOUR FATER MADE A FIRE. GRANDPA ALLEN WASSTUCK AT WORK ALL NIGHT ANWE ALL SELPT IN THE DEN. IM FINE HERE AND CLEAN AND EAT. NO INTERNET SHOPPING EMAIL IS ENOUGH WHAT DO YOU LEARN IN SCHOOL ARE YOU HAPPY LOVE BUBBE

She presses "send" again and pulls the chair back so she can see her toes. They have been bothering her. They are itchy.

She cannot bend over too far, so she eases herself out of the chair, back down on the floor, and pulls her leg up as close to her eyes as she can. She wants a magnifying glass. She wants eyes that come out of her knees. She wants to be able to bend over the way she used to, to touch the ground.

She has not been able to see things without a mirror since right before Allen died. She can no longer see her own pubic hair because of her stomach, and she can no longer turn her neck enough to look at the back of her shoulder. Even with her glasses, it is hard to see the scar she got when she was little from jumping on a bed and hitting her chin on the edge of it.

How silly, she thinks, for her scar to finally leave like that. That scar had bothered her for years, and now that it doesn't matter, now that she is on the floor stretching and squinting so she can see, there is no reason for her skin to even be here. Skin that causes her feet to itch, her hands to be dry. It is a nuisance. And then, beneath that, there are her joints and her bones, also a nuisance. She feels the absence of a strength she once had, as if the strength were a phantom pain from a lost limb. She hates her body, and wonders if death will make her only a mind, or a thought, or just dust.

Didn't your insides go first? Or did your outsides go first? Or did they go at the same time? No matter what, it is looking bad. If she lets herself think it she will think the worst; she is a glass-half-empty girl.

On her hands and knees, she crawls her way back toward the bathroom. Halfway there, she rests, lying down, her head on the carpet, where the dust has collected from no vacuuming since yesterday. It is comfortable. It is close to the computer. Why not? she thinks, making a pillow with her hands.

And then the dancers come toward her, holding hands. They are getting bigger as they run, all colors. They remind her of the old musicals she used to love, where the man held the woman as if she were as light as a piece of fabric. Effortless. She wishes they would stay. She tries to focus, putting her head down. But then they are gone and she is still on the floor, her knees bent, almost asleep.

10.

Abby is smoking alone outside the red doors when she hears someone. She drops her cigarette, but Chess opens the door.

"It's only me," he says, smiling, and she quickly picks it up.

"You scared me," she says, wiping the cigarette, then putting it back in her mouth. "I'm supposed to be in English and I'm failing."

"Really?" he says. "You're fucked!"

"No," she says, laughing. "I'll pass."

Abby has not spoken to Chess since the night on the lawn. After getting the note from Jenna, she figured this would be the way: she should walk around as if the boys had never sat on her lawn or watched her chug or touched her.

But it is not that way, apparently. New rule: You can talk to the friend of the boy who touched you, but you can't talk to the boy.

"I have a joint," Chess says, smirking, patting the pocket of his parka. "You want to go down to the Living Room and smoke?"

Abby has never been to the Living Room. Usually it would bother her that Chess is already a regular, but something about Chess makes her happy for him.

She'd stood on the Living Room's edge last week while waiting for Jenna to bum a cigarette and saw the famed couch, old red leather cracking white in places, as if a cloud were being suffocated, trying to get out.

Through the woods, while she waited for Jenna, she could see the table and the big oak stump, the "ashtray."

"Sure," Abby says.

No one owns the Living Room. It is a spot in the woods where some boys, years ago, carried their parents' basement furniture behind the school and put it beneath a bunch of ceiling-like trees. Those boys have long since graduated, and all the things that came afterward (the rug, the chairs, the fireplace poker) are now part of it.

Abby always hears people talk about the boys who have their own "seats" on the couch. There are stories about things that happen there, people who call it "the LR," and certain card games that are played on the glass table all coated with candle wax.

Chess motions to her and they begin to walk. Even though the Living Room is on the school grounds, it is too far out to worry about teachers. It is risky, though, in the winter when all the trees are bare.

It is perfect now, in the fall, the couch covered in leaves. They walk the sneakered path, over knobby tree veins. Chess seems to know each step, tells her to watch it where there are places to trip.

Abby prays no one is there. She thinks she will ask Chess about the city when they sit down. Perhaps she will ask him about how he played football there. And also, by the way, Chess, were you just born popular?

But up ahead she hears voices, and sees colors that are not red or brown or orange. They are pink and blue.

"Who's that?" Chess calls ahead.

"Who's *that*?" Jenna's voice singsongs back.

Chess runs ahead and jumps on the couch and Abby catches up to see Jenna with Alec, sitting on the couch too. Abby stands for a moment, then decides to sit across from them in one of the red leather chairs. The air smells horrible—moldy. Abby sees that Jenna is sitting on her book bag. She hadn't thought of that—how the furniture would be wet. It seems so strange that people ignore it.

"What are you guys up to?" Jenna says, smoking a cigarette and flicking the ashes on the ground.

Alec sits next to her. He does not look at Abby.

"Nada mucho," Chess says. He reaches in his pocket and takes out his cigarettes. She wonders if he is still going to take out his joint.

"We need to figure out a plan for Pep Rally," Jenna says, looking at Abby.

"I know," Abby says, but she is not sure what she means. She has never gone to the Pep Rally before, though she watched it, last year, from the woods. A big bonfire, the football boys in their helmets running through a poster as they are each announced by their last names. Cheering.

"I'm out," Chess says. He has the game the next day.

"I wasn't talking to you," Jenna says. "Was I?"

Chess smirks, sits, and pulls Jenna over so that she is sitting on his lap.

"I don't care who you were talking to," he says, tickling her.

Abby thinks how safe Chess makes her feel, even when he is holding someone else.

"Stop," Jenna says. "I'm going to pee on you!"

Chess stops.

"Jesus," she says, hitting his arm.

He puts both his hands beneath her armpits and starts tickling her again, laughing. He holds her in his arms, and Abby can see that she cannot get away.

"I'll pee!!" Jenna gasps, hysterical.

"OK, OK," he says, finally stopping.

Jenna leans over and falls across Alec, her lower half on Chess. Abby thinks it's amazing how much room a girl can take up.

"I know," Jenna says. "Let's get U-RINE!"

"That guy sounds like such a chump," Alec says.

"Yeah, get him with your wily ways," Chess says. "I'm sure you could get a lot out of him."

Jenna kicks him.

"Shut up," she says. "No, really. He'll get us some stuff. Don't you think?"

Abby isn't sure what stuff she is talking about. Certainly not drugs. It is so weird that Jorgen is someone they are talking about at the LR. She wishes he didn't exist.

"He'll totally get us alcohol," Jenna says. "Vodka!"

11.

The leaves on Simone's lawn have been raked, it looks like, recently. The grass is a nice green, Livia thinks, pulling up into the pebble driveway.

Next to her, in the front seat, are all the color and fabric samples she borrowed from a store downtown. She told the woman at the store they were for her, since they had helped her decorate her own house a few years ago. She needs to establish herself first before telling people about her business, especially people *in* the business, people like that.

Livia parks and picks up the heavy sample books. She is dressed for her job: flowy grey slacks, a black silky shirt tucked in, and a red scarf, untied, around her neck.

When she left the house, Jorgen was in the kitchen.

"Are you going somewhere specially?" Jorgen asked as she put on her coat. It was early, almost 11:15.

"Not specially," she said, smiling at him, then walking out the door.

She rings the doorbell to Simone's house, looking in the window on the side of the door. The foyer is empty, as it was before. It is true: Simone *is* waiting for her to decorate.

She hears the lock turn, the door handle move. Simone opens the door.

"Hello," she says and leans in to kiss Livia's cheek. Simone smells of Chanel No. 5, Livia's mother's old perfume.

Simone's cheek feels so soft.

"Let me help you with those," she says, taking half of the books that Livia is carrying and walking inside.

Livia begins to follow her into the kitchen. Simone is dressed in jeans and a white T-shirt. Livia is not sure if she is wearing a bra.

"Oh, I'm sorry," Simone says, looking down at Livia's feet. "Shoes?"

"My goodness," Livia says. "Of course." She takes off her heels and lines them up near the door next to Simone's (or her partner's) shoes. Seeing how large her shoes are next to the others makes her feels embarrassed.

"It's my day off," Simone says, walking toward the kitchen. She puts the sample books down on the kitchen counter and opens the fridge.

"Water? Coffee? Tea?" she asks.

"Coffee would be great," Livia says.

She watches as Simone takes the coffee grinds out of the fridge. The coffee label is French. The coffee brewer is stainless steel and new.

"Do you want something to eat?" Simone asks. "I was just going to have some pasta."

"Oh, no. I'm fine," Livia says. She has not eaten yet today—she will pick up something after. She does not like to eat in front of anyone.

Livia watches Simone go back to the fridge. She is sure, now, that she is not wearing a bra. When she turns her nipples stick out and show through: small and perky and seemingly brown.

"I've been really inspired by your house," Livia says. "I have some great ideas."

"Oh, that's wonderful," Simone says. "I felt inspired by it when we first saw it too."

She takes out a Tupperware full of pasta with vegetables and pours some into a small glass bowl. The perfect portion size. As big as a large man's fist.

Simone sits down at one of the kitchen island stools (ugly wood—needs to be replaced) and Livia sits next to her.

"OK, sorry, I'm ready," she says, picking up her fork. "I'm starving."

"Oh, no problem," Livia says.

Livia opens up to a bookmarked page in the first book to show her the paint samples (blues for the living room with names like "sea foam," "azure," and "cobalt"), and the matching fabric from the other book.

"This looks great," Simone says, pointing to certain colors, certain fabrics, with her unpolished, clean fingernail. "Gail will love this."

Livia thinks: when did she know she was a lesbian? Was she only a lesbian? Always? Do her patients know she is a lesbian? Do the neighbors know?

When Simone gets up to put her dish in the sink, Livia tries not to look at her breasts.

12.

There are ants in the carpet.

All this time she thought her house was clean. Now, lying on her bed of blankets on the hall carpet, Headie sees what she has been missing.

She tries hard to focus. Sometimes she can't tell if it is her eyes playing tricks. She is unsure if the carpet fibers are really moving. She moves her hand back and forth, but the light in the hall is dim—there are no windows. It is the good and the bad thing about sleeping there.

Headie closes her eyes. She thinks about Millie, whom she hasn't heard from in a couple of days. She will email her.

Headie's toes hurt. They are scrunched up from years of being high-heeled. She tries to flex them every day in her white house slippers, but time has snuggled her toes together into a crooked rail.

Headie does not like to look at her feet. A long time ago they were her most perfect part. When they were first together, she let Allen slip off her shoes, but after a few years she hid them beneath their blankets.

How could it be that she has ugly toes? She thinks of the Chinese women who bound their feet, and the dancers who wrap their feet. Women who soak their feet in hot baths, and women who paint their toenails.

She wishes she took care of her feet, treated them as two small babies, putting them into warm water to clean them, individually, where she could see.

Headie opens her eyes and turns over to watch the ants. She likes to imagine squashing them every time she moves.

Allen loved her feet. He would die all over again if he was alive now and knew they had ants.

It is strange to think of Allen alive again. When she pictures him coming back to life, she always pictures the young Allen. The young Allen, the first Allen, the Allen she knew before she married Gene. The Allen who knew her when she was young.

That Allen made it happen. And when it happened, it was not romance. It did not happen in a swan bed, where she imagined it would happen; it did not even happen in a bedroom.

It happened only once and it was not enough.

Afterward when she saw him in synagogue with his wife, Headie would try to catch his eye. He ignored her, walked right by her without even a glance. (When Headie saw Monica Lewinsky on TV telling everyone how the President used to wear the ties she gave him when he gave a speech, Headie liked that, and wished that Allen had done the same. That was a perfect way.)

Headie was twenty-six, an old maid, dusting, getting ready to close the store where she had worked since she was out of high school. It was a man's store when she first began working—it was a woman's store now.

Allen walked in and smiled.

"She'll never be a Jew," she had heard women say, even after Allen's wife had converted and they were married. She had beautiful blonde hair, which she wore low in a bun. She had thick ankles, but otherwise there was nothing you could say was not pretty on her. She was beautiful in a way only a shiksa could be.

"I need a scarf," Allen said that evening in the store, only fifteen minutes until she was supposed to close. He looked her in the eye. He had slicked-back black hair and a long face with big dimples. He wore a suit like he was going somewhere, but he took off his jacket and laid it on the bench, as if he didn't mind being late.

Headie knew that salesgirls were supposed to be chatty, and with the women she was, but she did not ask Allen about his wife or how he liked being back at home, working with his father. He had gone to a different high school than she had, and he was older, but she had always seen him in synagogue. He had left for years while he went to college, then law school, and then came home with the shiksa to get married and work at his father's firm.

Headie led him over to the scarves on the rack. There were different colors and patterns, all flowy and gauzy. Her favorite, which she would secretly try on sometimes after the boss had left, had tulips on it in a sea of green grass.

"How about this one?" he asked. He picked up her favorite scarf with the tulips and held it in front of him like a sheet he was about to fold.

Headie was close enough to him to see his sleeveless undershirt through his button-down. He was so large.

"Here," he said. "Try it!"

Headie was twenty-six and had never been touched.

He put it around her neck and tied it, then stood back while she looked down, her face hot and surely red.

"Yes, it will look great with my wife's coloring," he said. Headie's own (dark and pale) was the exact opposite.

Headie was wearing her pencil skirt, her high-heel shoes, her silky blouse buttoned up to the top: her work clothes. She had dark brown frizzy hair, but she pulled it back into a chignon. Each morning she spent time poufing her hair up to cover the flatness of her head in the back.

"Headra," he said, pointing his finger at her as if she had just appeared. "*That's* your name."

"Yes," she said.

She wrapped the scarf in tissue paper, folding it gently, sadly, three times over.

"You know," he said, "would you take it out and try it on again? I just want to be sure."

Headie stopped and reversed her three folds, not looking up, just taking the scarf out and putting it around her neck. He reached over the counter to tie it in the front, and she felt his fingertip touch her neck.

He moved the scarf, putting the knot to the side, then the middle. He stopped shifting it and put his hand flat, below it, on her clavicle.

"Do you have a bathroom?" he asked, taking his hand away.

Headie nodded and began to point.

"Can you show it to me?" he asked.

"Sure," Headie said, turning and walking down past the dresses, the underwear and girdles, to the back, past the storage room. She could hear her shoes click and his click behind her. Usually she liked how tall and slim her shoes made her feel, but now she wondered how she looked from behind, if she seemed big.

As she turned the corner to the bathroom he pressed her against the storage cabinet.

Headie gasped.

He pulled the chain of the light on the ceiling, making it dark and hard to see his face.

He pulled her skirt up quickly, then unzipped his fly, pushing himself against her.

"Ha!" he said, trying to get inside.

She bit her lip. He did not kiss her. It hurt but she liked it. She thought about each place he was putting his hands.

She could feel the storage closet shake, all the shoes and old accessories moving inside, making noise. She listened to their rhythm as his first thrusts, rough and fast, turned slower and even. She held on to the top of his shoulders and moved against him. She leaned back and looked at his face. He opened his eyes.

"There you go," he said, thrusting harder again. She held on as he pushed her against the closet, the empty shoes shaking and dancing as she opened up for a married man and joined them.

In the morning, Headie climbs out of the hall, and to the table for breakfast. Yesterday she decided not to plug the phone in. She kept the computer plugged in instead—she hates to plug and unplug. She watches the trees outside the yellow curtained windows. It will snow and snow in a few months. It always does, but she is used to it, and has prepared for the winter. She does not eat as much as she used to, and she freezes things. Most of the time it is hard to tell what the food is until she takes it out of the baggies.

Headie used to cook meals for Allen, but they were simple—he liked meat. She is not a chef and she does not bake. She does not know how to. She does not want to, either. Once you start baking, everyone expects you to keep going, to get better and better, to make bigger cakes.

13.

When Abby sees Jorgen walk into the kitchen, she is annoyed. She is sure that he heard more than one set of footsteps, sure that he has come up from the basement because he knows Jenna is here.

"Would you like a schnack?" he says, wearing his red tracksuit.

He looks like he has just woken up, his usually parted hair messy. It looks better this way, but he is still gross.

Jenna and Abby take off their coats and sit down at the small kitchen table.

"What do you want?" Abby asks.

"What do you guys have?" Jenna asks.

"We have fruit," Jorgen says, "and frozen yogurt."

"No ice cream, Jorgen?" Jenna says, putting her arms out on the table and leaning her head down on them. She is dressed in tight jeans, a black shirt that buttons low in the front, and black beaded dangly earrings to match.

"No," says Jorgen.

Abby bites the side skin of her nail—a bad habit. She has bloody nail beds and leaves little trails of blood on book pages from all her skin picking.

Abby watches as Jenna gets up and walks to the freezer. In her high boots she is almost as tall as Jorgen.

"I don't believe you," Jenna says, opening the freezer and leaning into it so from where Abby sits it looks like her head has disappeared into the cool fridge mist.

"No, really. We don't," Jorgen says. Abby hates that he says "we" like it's his ice cream that isn't there.

Jenna takes the frozen yogurt out and looks at the label. Jorgen gets two bowls out of the cabinet.

"I don't want any," Abby says, and Jorgen turns and looks at her.

"Oh, I know," Jorgen says. "I want some too."

Jenna brings the peach yogurt to the table and sits down next to Abby. Jorgen sits on Jenna's other side. He scoops the yogurt out for both of them, smiling at Jenna when he hands her the bowl.

Abby wishes this didn't have to happen. Beer was easy; so was pot. Why was vodka such a struggle? Why didn't anyone's parents have full bottles that they wouldn't notice were gone?

Abby watches as Jenna leans over, her lip against the inside scoop of the spoon. She can see Jenna's tongue. She watches Jorgen watch Jenna.

Abby wonders if it's time for her to leave. This is part of the plan.

"You'll know when," Jenna told her on their walk home from school. "Just say you have to go to the bathroom."

"I'm gonna go to the bathroom," Abby says now, getting up and walking past the dining room into the hall. Right outside the bathroom she stops, listening, then goes in and turns on the water. She steps out again and shuts the door, then tiptoes back so that she can see into the kitchen.

Jenna is kneeling on her chair now, leaning farther toward Jorgen.

"Yeah, I think it's going to be great," she says.

Jorgen nods. "In Sweden we have a similar party," he says.

"You guys say '*skol*' right?" Jenna says.

Abby wonders how she knows this.

"Yes, we say '*skol*'!" Jorgen says, lifting up his spoon as if he is clinking glasses. Some of his yogurt falls onto his other hand.

Abby watches as Jenna takes her finger and swipes the yogurt off his hand, then licks her finger. She does it all in one smooth motion. Off Jorgen's hairy hand.

"We say 'cheers'!" she says, lifting up her hand, then tipping her spoon so that yogurt falls onto her own hand.

"Whoops!" she says. Abby watches as Jenna looks down at the orange melting on her skin.

"Cheers!" Jorgen says, taking a napkin and wiping her hand off.

Abby watches Jorgen. His face is red, as if he is hot or embarrassed.

"Yeah, so," Jenna says, "we need to get stuff to party with."

"Oh, I can party," Jorgen says.

"No, no," Jenna laughs and Abby tries not to. "Stuff."

"Oh, oh!" Jorgen says. "I guess it is not for older people."

"No, just students," Jenna says. "But maybe we can sneak you in . . ."

"Really?" Jorgen says.

This is not the plan.

"Maybe," Jenna says. She takes another bite of the yogurt and moves her legs to sit on her ass again. She pulls her chair close to Jorgen, straddling the seat, then says, almost whispering, "But we need your help."

Watching Jenna, Abby can't believe the way pubic hair is ignored. This thought comes up each time she imagines doing anything with a boy. Abby grew pubic hair early, which made her feel strange from the start.

Jenna touches Jorgen's chest and Abby worries about Jorgen's pubic hair. How will Jenna not laugh? How can anyone think that pubic hair is OK? It scares her, the thought that sex makes you ignore these things. Sex makes you open up without laughing. It makes you grunt and not blush. Abby has seen a porno before where no one even had pubic hair. And no one says anything about it. And no one is laughing.

Abby watches Jenna ignore Jorgen's pubic hair. She watches Jenna ignore her own.

Abby watches and thinks about the pubic hair she first got: soft and light, not like what it has turned into. Her mother thought she was too young—she was only eight—and took her to the doctor when she saw it. The doctor said that Abby was just hairy.

Abby thinks how relieved she is now that she does not have the hairy problem anymore. Or rather, that the hairy problem is manageable, can be removed.

Abby had been hairy for so long. The kids had already begun to tease her before seventh grade because of her hair in general, but then she moved here and got the part of the stepmother in the school play of *Cinderella*, and things got worse.

Abby got the role because she could yell. She yelled and yelled at her audition, sang "I Felt Nothing" from *A Chorus Line* for her audition song, and stared down every blonde girl they had her up against as Cinderella on the stage.

After she got the part, she got quieter. At the third rehearsal, the director asked her in front of everyone: "Where's the stepmother who auditioned for me?"

This made her worry.

Still, she had a hard time getting back to her "yelling" place. Her mother yelled and never seemed to have a hard time doing it. She didn't have "up" and "down" yelling days. It was always in the same pitch: up the stairs she yelled for dinner, outside she yelled for Abby to come in, and down the hallway she yelled at her Dad when he came home.

Abby wanted to yell. She just felt intimidated. Already the girls who didn't have good parts, the pretty girls who were the dancers in the play and wore black spandex bodysuits with fairy wings and did a dance when the Fairy Godmother sang "Bibitty Bobitty Boo," for what seemed like no reason, had started to get mean.

In the locker room, changing for gym, the girls would sing the songs from the show together. They sang all of the songs: Cinderella's, the king's, and then the stepmother's: Abby's. One day, when Abby was singing along to her song, practicing, as if she was on stage (the show was only two weeks away), everyone went quiet. She continued a few words, before hearing the laughter. She was singing alone.

Pre–dress rehearsal she was nervous, but opening night she felt almost sexy. She changed into her costume from her day clothes in the chorus room. For a minute, at school, she was only in her tights and bra. She quickly put on her long stepmother dress.

The high school girls who helped out with the show put makeup on her in the art room, the foundation orange and cakey. It had a certain smell and had been used for years and years. Even the boys had to wear it.

After the senior was done with her, she held up a mirror: Abby's skin looked smooth, stocking-like, and she looked pretty with all the eye shadow and dark lipstick. She felt different.

Right before they closed the auditorium for the first act, in her long gold-flecked dress, her black hair on top of her head in what her mother called "a mean beehive," long white gloves on her hands that she tried not to touch her face with, Abby's stomach began to hurt.

The high school girls were down by the doors, having their last cigarettes before the show started, so she went to the teacher's bathroom, past the art room. The teacher's bathroom: one stall, and usually no one in it.

Abby's stomach was hurting in a way that made her double over. She tried to think of what she had eaten, think of who would go on for her if she fainted or died. All those girls who sang her song in the locker room would have loved to have her part, but she did not have an understudy. She had yelled the loudest.

In the stall she put her head between her knees. She was sweating, as if her body was poisoned. She did not have a watch. She had diarrhea.

She worried about this often: going on long car rides where neither of her parents was driving, eating out at a restaurant, or in school. What was happening now, her body, disguised in her stepmother suit, her white gloves becoming more and more orange with foundation as she wiped stray hairs from her wet face, was exactly what she dreaded.

"ABBYYYYYY!!!!" she heard a herd of tap-shoed footsteps coming down the hall. She looked out the slots of the stall. She farted loudly. The girls walked in.

"ABBYYYYYY!!!" they yelled. "Come on! The show's starting!!!!!"

Abby tried to get up and wipe as fast as she could.

"Mr. Polumbo is playing the opening music for a SECOND time!!!"

"I'm coming!" Abby said, flushing quickly.

She ran back with the girls, in through the back-stage and out to the lights. She began to sing.

After the first song's applause, Abby went backstage.

"Something smells," she heard the prince whisper. His voice was only half changed (he was the only one who could hit the high notes), and he had to wear tights.

She heard some more whisper-laughs and went out into the hall. Something *did* stink.

She went into the art room where the dancers were waiting for their one big scene, perfecting their makeup and talking. Abby walked in and sat down at one of the tables, making sure she hadn't sweat off all of her makeup.

"What the fuck smells?" said Caroline, a mean, small girl who always wore headbands. She smelled the air, then looked over at Abby.

"Smells like shit," another girl said.

Abby concentrated on her makeup, trying to get her eye shadow to look the same on both eyes. She didn't have much time.

"Ew! Look at her glove!!!!"

Abby stopped and sniffed. She looked in the mirror. There was shit on her right-handed glove.

"Ugh," Abby said, quickly taking the glove off and running back to the bathroom. She threw both gloves in the sink and turned on the water. She could hear the loud tap shoes of the dancing girls getting closer.

"Ass juice!" she heard, right before the door opened and the girls looked in the sink, pretending to gag.

"Feces!" Caroline said.

Jenna kneels and puts Jorgen in her mouth. Jorgen's pubic hair is reddish. He pushes her head down.

Abby is not sure that this was supposed to happen. She tries to think back, watching Jorgen's fingers—fingers that will make her dinner tonight—rake through Jenna's soft brown hair. Jenna's free hand seems to be trying to hold on to the tiled floor.

Jorgen pushes Jenna's head down. It seems mean—Jenna's face is red, her eyes shut tight. Suddenly he groans, done. Jenna lifts her head and swallows.

Jorgen quickly pulls his sweatpants up. That's the good thing about not having to button or zip, Abby thinks, going back into the bathroom and washing her hands: you can act like nothing has happened.

14.

To: headragoldstein@aol.com
From: livia@liviathedesigner.com

Dear Headie-
Things are great here. I'm really concentrating on that new client I wrote you about. She has a huge old house on the Neck. I am doing a full design restoration.
I'm planning on keeping the walls of the larger rooms neutral, and warm the place with brighter colored accents (I'm focusing on blues and greens). I'll try to send you a

"What the fuck is this?" Jeffrey asks, walking into the study. He is dressed in his work clothes, holding a white garbage bag.

"What?" Livia says, swiveling around the desk chair to see him.

"This!" he says, putting the bag close to her face.

Inside are soggy cigarettes with blades of grass still stuck to them, beer cans still dripping drops of beer.

"Gross," Livia says. "Get that away, Jeffrey, it's smelling up the room."

Jeffrey sits down on the couch. Livia watches him as he looks back in the bag.

"It's cigarettes and beer cans," Livia says.

"From our front lawn," Jeffrey says. "I found this out by the road."

Livia turns back to the computer. Sometimes she wishes her own mother was still alive. Maybe she could have gotten a computer too.

picture of the outside of the house. Right now the inside is mostly bare. It is a perfect palette for m

"Liv!" Jeffrey says, standing up and bringing the bag next to her again.

"What?" Livia says.

"We have to talk about this! Whose are these?" Livia looks up—it is dusk and the sun is shining in small stripes through the almost-closed blinds from the backyard. Jeffrey never understands decorating or good lighting. He never thinks to open the blinds.

"I don't know," Livia says, and suddenly fears that he thinks they are hers. She started smoking for a period of time again (she had smoked in her twenties but stopped when she met Jeffrey—he hated it) after Abby started first grade, and she always worried that he would catch her.

For a while she smoked in her car, sometimes just sitting there, parked in the driveway, when it was too cold.

Livia washed her hair and brushed her teeth before he came home so Jeffrey didn't smell her. She was sure he never suspected anything, but still, she ended up quitting before he accused her; she couldn't stand watching herself smoke in the rearview mirror—looking below her eyes at the thin-as-tissue skin covered in her smoke. She looked at her lips and remembered when they had no creases in them at all.

She ended up smoking her last cigarette, then emptying the car ashtray in the Dumpster. Abby was in sixth grade then and they were planning on moving. That was that.

"They're not mine," she says.

"Of course they aren't yours," he says, wrapping the bag around and around at the top and making a knot.

Livia swivels the chair back to face the computer. She wishes she had decided to stay in the bedroom instead of moving her work to the desk before Jeffrey came home.

y ideas.

How is Millie? Is it getting very cold there? It's been mild here so far.

"Liv!" Jeffrey says, "What are we going to do?" Livia stops typing.

"I don't know," she says.

"Do you think it's that new friend of hers?" Jeffrey says.

She hadn't thought of that; didn't think of Abby, even. She had thought of other people's kids or gardeners on breaks. For a second she had thought of Jorgen.

"You think they're from Abby?" she asks, turning around and watching as he undresses.

"Who else would they be from?" he says, hanging up his suit in his closet.

She cannot imagine her daughter smoking. Abby is not a smoking girl. Livia had been *that* kind of girl. Before she went to college she had already had sex with five boys. She had dyed her hair jet-black and cut it short and then grew it out two-toned.

Livia imagines Abby drinking a beer.

"It's that girl," Jeffrey says.

"Jenna?" Livia says.

Livia met Jenna briefly after coming home from Simone's. She and Abby were in the living room watching TV. She seemed nice. A pretty girl. Jenna looks like a real teenager. Abby seems much younger.

Livia quickly saves the draft of her email and goes to a decorating Web site. She can't concentrate on writing with Jeffrey talking.

Livia sighs. "Are you going to say something?"

"Of course!" he says. "Of course—Livia—don't you realize this is a problem? You really need to grow up here. Our daughter is drinking and smoking, for God's sake! What's wrong with you?"

Jeffrey has not told her to grow up for ages. When they were younger he gave her the same line. He told her she was a spoiled brat and a child.

When Abby was first born, and Livia was overwhelmed and bored, he brought home books on mothering. She sometimes tried to read them (occasionally, guiltily, she used earplugs to block out the baby's crying) but ended up falling asleep instead.

She had breastfed like they had decided. She had decorated Abby's baby room. She dressed Abby up when they went anywhere, and when her hair was long enough she put it in pigtails.

When Abby was first born, Livia tried to picture other women doing what she was. She thought about other women surviving it, surviving worse. She thought of Auschwitz, made herself imagine being in the camp, closing her eyes and feeling hunger. Then she would open her eyes and try to feel relieved. All she had was a baby girl sucking (and sucking and sucking) her.

But sometimes Livia watched Abby sleep. Sometimes she made Abby smile, kissed her and licked her lips, just to see what it felt like.

Sometimes, when Abby was awake in her crib, just looking around, at the ceiling, at the mobile, her eyes unfocused, Livia reached down and held her tiny hands. She put her face close to her daughter's and tried to imagine what she was thinking.

Still, there was the sucking, the crying, the drain. At first Livia did not tell Jeffrey about how hard it was. She had agreed to a child (telling him and everyone during those nine long months that she couldn't wait!), and had looked forward to staying at home without being expected to work. No one was going to make her feel guilty for being in bed all day. She would be a Mother.

Each day Livia washed her face and put on makeup before Jeffrey came home in the evening. She had Abby's diaper changed and ready. But one day Jeffrey surprised them and came home for lunch. He caught Livia sleeping with the earplugs, and Abby crying, unheard, in the next room.

From then on Livia cried. She cried each night when Jeffrey came home. She knew she looked unlovable, crying the way she did. She looked unlovable and so she was. She cried with her daughter.

"You're a mother, Liv," Jeffrey told her, whispering as Abby fell asleep, her pink lips dislodging from Livia's sore nipple.

Later, when he was exhausted with her, angry with her, had had enough, he phrased it differently.

"You have to grow up," he said.

Livia has grown up a lot since then.

"Well," she says. "What are you going to say?"

"We have to be in this together," Jeffrey says, now fully dressed in his sweats. He picks up the plastic bag from where he put it on the floor. "We need to confront her with this."

"What?" Livia says. "You've got to be kidding me, Jeffrey. You're making it like a police investigation. It's just some beer . . . "

Livia is distracted by the salmon-pink light coming in the room. She gets up and walks to the window, opening the blind so that she can see the sunset.

"You have to confront this in the beginning," he says.

Livia stares outside and breathes deeply. Leaves are falling off the trees. The light is so nice.

15.

Headie crawls into the living room on top of the rug that covers the carpet. The rug is the same shade of blue as the carpet, accented in browns and other blues.

The blinds are closed. The pile is soft.

She reaches for the end of the rug, holds on, and begins to roll. The rug rolls around her. She keeps rolling until the rug stops.

She is like a pig in a blanket with no room to move. All wrapped up she is warm and safe, trapped with the smell. She likes it, and wishes they had thought to carpet the walls.

Millie has wallpaper in her kitchen that is textured with soft fabric in the shape of lemons. When she goes over, Headie always looks around the lemon-yellow phone where the fabric lemons have turned grayish from fingerprints. Years and years of Millie talking.

All rolled up, Headie pushes her arm back and begins to roll out again. Going out is fast and easy: the stiff rug unrolls itself. It rolls her onto the carpet, letting her out of its embrace.

Headie looks up at the ceiling but lets her eyes see on the side. There they are: the dancers. They dance quickly, colorfully, doing that dance Gene had done. She cannot remember the name. Some funny name . . . Once, in their living room, in the first and only house they owned, Gene had turned on the music, dancing like he sometimes did. He was such a good dancer—his first love, his fiancée, Lilac, had been his dance partner. Headie was no dancer, but in their living room Gene looked like he was waiting for her to join him. Headie put out her arms for him to lead her, but he shook his head and sipped his scotch.

"No," he said. "Show me how you dance by yourself."

They were about to leave for a dinner party.

"Come on," he said. "Show me."

Because he never asked for much, and because, mostly, he was a sweet man, and because she never had any more children and because she never really loved him, she stood in the living room and slipped off her shoes and held her hands together. She swayed from side to side, slowly, looking down.

"That's how?" he asked. She always refused to dance quickly with him and always made him find another partner, but slow dances were fine; slow ones he moved her.

"Listen to the beat, Headie," he said, still watching her, and she gave a quick hip shake each time she swayed one way, another little shake when she swayed the other.

She looked up, clapped her hands together.

"You ready?" she said, done.

Gene never asked her to dance for him after that, and Headie was glad. But when she was alone, in her stockinged feet, she turned on the radio and shook herself, letting her head bob, her knees bend, her hands jiggle in the air. She wasn't sure anyone danced this way, and she never looked in the mirror. But it felt good, and she twirled around the house, sometimes bumping into things, careful to do it only lightly. She never broke anything; she never left a clue.

Now, lying on the floor, Headie watches the dancers twirling, still colorful, still faceless. She tries to pretend they aren't there, pretend she doesn't care if they are dancing or not. But this makes them dance more.

When Headie lets herself concentrate on the dancers, she thinks too much about how she cannot jump around the way she used to. She knows what is next.

In Headie's bedroom closet there hangs the pink and white nightgown she plans to be buried in when she dies. She wrote a note that she pinned to the hanger that says to whoever finds her dead: "BURY ME IN THIS!"

The nightgown is flannel with small pink roses and a paler pink background. The collar has white ruffles that hide her neck. Allen bought it for her for their last Chanukah before he died. She had only worn it once, the last time they tried to make love. He was too weak, then, to lift up her dress from behind the way he used to. Even with Viagra. So she licked his flaccid penis. It was enough.

She hugged him while he lay there. When he died, she decided that the nightgown would be the right thing to wear when they laid her in the plot next to his.

No one knows, but Headie brings the nightgown everywhere she sleeps. She brings it each time she goes to visit her son, and to all the funerals that are far away. She brings it when she sleeps anywhere other than her own bed.

Each time it is the same: she folds the nightgown up, always above her underwear but below all the other clothes, near the bottom of her suitcase, in a see-through plastic bag. Then, when she gets wherever she is going, she hangs it up right next to what she has brought to wear while she is still alive.

She knows that other people wear fancy clothes in their coffins. They wear the clothes that she has seen them wearing the week before at synagogue.

At each shivah she makes sure that she takes one helping of tuna salad and that she says her condolences before she asks the closest family member what it is their dead are buried in.

No one, so far, has told her that the dead person is wearing a nightgown. It is a surprise to her that no one else thought of it. Flannel keeps you warm. A nightgown makes perfect sense.

Lately, Headie has not thought about the nightgown as much. Wrapped in plastic, it is only in the corner of her eye. On the floor, it is out of her line of vision. Off to the side, a lot like death itself.

To: headragoldstein@aol.com
From: Millieschwartz@aol.com

Headie—
I fell on the ice. I have been trying to call you but your line just rings. I guess you really like the Internet. Now the

doctor says to stay inside in bed and rest. I am resting. So no
synagogue. Fun to write! We will write to each other!
   Love,
   Millie

To: millieschwartz@aol.com
From: headragoldstein@aol.com

MILLIE ILOVE THE COMPUTER THANK YOU
IM SORRY THAT YOU FELEL DONT WORRY
ABOUT ME THOUGH. I AM VERY GOOD AND
CLEANING. WINTER SOON LOVE HEADIE

16.

Sometimes Abby hears walking at night, downstairs. It is her mother's steps, she is certain. Loud steps that she doesn't realize she needs to muffle. Her mother's feet often wake her, the way they pound the floors.

Her father falls asleep quickly. Sometimes when they are all watching TV in the evening he will begin dozing. They have to wake him to get him to bed.

At night, when Abby wants to go to sleep, she imagines herself spinning backwards, as if her whole body is on a hamster wheel and she is holding on to the top, her feet buckled into the bottom. She likes to think of herself tied up this way, and when she can't fall asleep she imagines that there is a man there, and that the wheel is still, and that her feet are buckled differently.

Tonight, while Abby is trying to spin, there is a knock at her bedroom door.

"It's your father," he says.

Abby tells him he can come in. He steps into her room holding a plastic bag.

The carpet in Abby's room is a different color than in the hall. The carpet is separated by a brass edge. It is like this in all the carpeted rooms in the house, as if each room is a separate state on a map.

Her father is in his after-work clothes—sweatpants and his v-neck undershirt. His chest hair peeks out of the top. He is hairy—it is where she gets her hairiness from, she is sure. She loves her father but she is sure it is his fault she is ugly.

Abby's father sits on her old blue desk chair and leans forward, silently. He does not smile or kiss her forehead.

"What's this?" he asks, leaning forward and opening the bag. Abby looks in: cigarettes, beer, and blades of grass. She can smell the night on her lawn.

"We need to talk about this, Abby," her father says. His voice is calm and soft. Whenever he kisses her forehead his lips are cool.

Abby fingers the edge of her comforter, waiting for her father to say what's next. This has not happened before; the anger in their house was never thrown at Abby. There was never room for it.

"So you're mad at me?" she asks.

He takes the bag back, ties the ends, and lets it drop on the floor next to him.

"If I ever see you smoking, I don't care where, I will take the cigarette out of your mouth and punish you."

This is not a tone she has heard from her father before. It is not the tone he uses to yell at her mother. It is not the tone she hears him with on the phone, making work calls. This is a new tone. If she closed her eyes and listened, she would not even recognize him.

"I'm sorry," Abby says.

"I'm disappointed," her father says. She watches him look down at the carpet, back at the bag. She wishes he hadn't shown it to her the way he did. Why couldn't he just have said something? It seems mean, that bag on the floor.

"I'm sorry," she says again. She wishes the bag would disappear and he would hug her.

"If this happens again, I'll have to ground you." His new tone has a shake in it. His voice seems to keep getting deeper.

"OK," Abby says.

"Your mother feels the same way, but she thought it would be too much if both of us came up here."

"OK, Dad," she says, truly sorry, reaching across her bed to her father, her arms out, as if her bed was a sinking boat.

He gets up from the chair and leans down and hugs her. It makes her sad: he smells like the night on the lawn.

"I'm sorry," she says, and he kisses her forehead.

"Good night, hon," he says, picking up the bag.

When he goes to the door Abby's heart begins pounding. The door closes, and, alone, she is back on her sinking boat.

Jenna has gotten them everything; there is no turning back now. The bottle is under Abby's bed. Jorgen made them wait in the car at the liquor store and came back with lemon-flavored vodka.

"Why did you get lemon?" Jenna asked from the front seat. She got the front seat now.

"Oh, you don't like the lemon?" Jorgen said.

"It's fine," Jenna said, and passed the bottle back to Abby.

Beneath her bed the bottle sits next to two packs of cigarettes. They are covered by her bed's blue dust ruffle.

She can never see that face on her father; she can never hear that new voice again. She will not tell Jenna about her father or her father about Jenna. She straps herself in the middle, decided. There is no other way.

The hamster wheel spins. She lets the man buckle her feet and her hands. He is up her shirt, down her pants, his hands everywhere, then inside her. And she is helpless, she is trapped, and he knows what he is doing. He is safe, he is cool—but not like a father at all.

17.

A bag of chips and pre-made onion dip sit on Livia's lap while she drives to town. She has work to do.

Livia keeps the dip balanced between her legs and uses one hand to drive, the other to scoop. When she eats she is never sure she is full until she is finished. She always eats until her plate is clean.

When she was younger she used to say she had an "efficient system," but now her system has changed. She will eat more today and not have to go to the bathroom until tonight or tomorrow morning. Her body does not run the way it used to; it does not run without her. Now it actually reacts to what she does.

Livia stops eating when she gets to town. She wipes her face and puts on lipstick at the light, then parks near the decorating store. Her phone rings just as she is about to get out of the car. It is Simone, written "SI-MONES" in her caller ID.

"Hello?" she says, as if she does not know who it is.

"Hi, it's Simone."

"Oh, hi Simone. How are you?"

"I'm fine. Fine. How are you?"

Livia tells her that she is just on her way to the design store.

"Oh, perfect. I showed the colors to Gail and she's interested in seeing some more options. She was wondering what you thought of mauve-ish type colors . . ."

"Oh," Livia says. She tries to think of what she thinks about this. "I have some ideas. Let me get some things together and I'll call you."

"Sounds great," Simone says. "Would you be able to come by tomorrow? Gail is kind of anxious . . . "

Simone says that seven would be great if she could do it, and Livia says that that sounds fine.

She hangs up, thinking of mauves, and looks out the window. At the intersection she sees what looks like Abby, her black hair flying out the passenger side of an open red Jeep. Livia puts her hand up to wave but she does not turn around. The car stops at the light and Livia watches her twist her hair and then drop it down her back. With her hair behind her ears, Livia can see Abby's face: she is smiling.

The driver is a handsome boy with brownish hair covering his forehead. He taps his thumb and pinky on the side of the car, a cigarette smoking in his fingers. He nods his head hard so that his hair flops. He takes a drag and smiles.

Livia does not try to wave again. She sits in her seat and watches her daughter. Abby looks pretty smiling. Sometimes people have said she looks a bit like Livia, but when she was little people mostly said that she looked like her father.

She watches as Abby takes a drag of her cigarette, then flicks it out the side of the Jeep. The light changes but her cigarette stays lit and smoking in the street.

Livia follows the back of the Jeep through her rearview mirror. Already Abby's hair has become untwisted, flailing around her, out of control.

When Livia was younger, when she wanted more of Jeffrey, she imagined what Abby would be like and pictured her daughter as two shoes: one shoe for herself, one for Jeffrey. There was only one shoe for each foot. Each shoe the same size, walkable with the same heel, but different brands, different colors, different in every other way.

Abby, their child, was the wearer of the two shoes, Livia used to think, the wearer-outer of them, the thing that made them fit.

Livia leans down and puts her onion dip and chips in the plastic bag they came in. She ties the bag tightly and flips down the visor mirror to make sure there are no crumbs on her face, that her lipstick looks the way it is supposed to.

She pushes her hair back. Abby has her widow's peak. It was one of the first things Jeffrey pointed to after Abby was born.

Livia gets out of the car and throws away the bag on her way into the decorating store. As usual, the owner is busy with a client. This is fine with Livia: she heads straight to the back for the paint swatches.

Livia looks at mauves. She read online that if there is nature in view from a window in the house that a decorator should emphasize it with color. Gail is wrong. Mauve is not the color of the sea. It does not reflect nature.

Mauve is the color that she picked out for Abby's carpet when they first moved.

Abby of the widow's peak, Livia thinks. Her daughter.

Smoking Abby, she thinks. For some reason it seems funny.

Livia's own parents smoked, so when she began smoking, no one noticed. The house already smelled, but she liked the idea of opening her windows, so she did. When she was a teenager she would lean her head out in the spring and summer and let her hair blow. It was romantic.

She liked to picture herself like a painting she had seen somewhere. By Dalí. Not one of his normal, dreamy paintings. This painting was of the back of his sister, looking out at the ocean through a window. Livia's mother had told her that the reason you couldn't see his sister's face was because she was ugly and Dali didn't want to paint her.

The girl in the painting wore a sailor-style dress. Livia did not have a sailor-style dress. Still, she imagined herself looking sweet from behind, as if a man would be pleased if he opened the door without knocking.

Livia looks at the mauves. Dark mauve (plum), light mauve (applewood), and in-between mauve (light fig). She hates them all.

She looks toward the purples. Perhaps she could fool them. Fool Gail.

Livia picks out some of the more purplish mauves. She takes some more sea foam samples too, just in case.

She goes over to the fabric swatch books to find something to match.

She'll bring the samples tomorrow. She hopes that Jeffrey did not make plans or tell her plans that she has forgotten. Either way, she will tell him it is business. She wants a pool.

She will bring some appropriate wine. She will ask at the wine store for something full-bodied, red. Not white and sloppy drunk.

Livia waves goodbye to the decorator ladies and walks to the car with the books. She gets in and begins driving, trying to open a chip bag with one hand and her teeth.

It is her second binge of the day, but she feels anxious, worried that Jeffrey will get angry. The other night, when Livia had not gone up the stairs to punish her daughter with him, he was annoyed.

Instead, Livia had waited for Jeffrey's footsteps to stop at the top of the stairs, then walked out of her room on tiptoe. She went down the hall (Jorgen was in the basement, thank God) and walked silently up the carpeted steps.

Through the tiny crack in Abby's door, Livia could see the back of her husband sit down and put the white plastic bag next to him.

She could hear the tone in his voice change, but not what he said. She watched as Abby looked at her father. Her face looked sad, strange.

She watched her daughter's face as he became quieter. She knew what this meant. Abby's face was like her own.

Livia drives to the town green that looks out on the Sound to eat her chips. She does not want to go home yet. She parks and looks at the playground, some teenagers sitting on the monkey bars, one mother with a small child in the sandbox.

When Abby was little Livia would take her to a park in Philadelphia to feed the ducks in the pond. Then one day, when Livia wasn't holding her, Abby accidentally fell in the water. Livia went right in the water to get her, but Abby had scraped her face, and when Jeffrey came home that night and saw her he told Livia that she could no longer take Abby to the park.

Still, she did. When Abby talked about the park to Jeffrey, Livia would tell him that she was confused. She was only three then, small and happy. Her scrapes went away quickly, although for a few weeks after, when people asked, Livia told them that she had left her with a babysitter and look what happened.

Livia sits in the parking lot, rolls down the window, looks at the water, and eats.

The first time she disappointed her husband they were sitting at the breakfast table in their first apartment. It was a few years into their marriage. She had said she was thinking she had changed her mind.

"Now?" Jeffrey yelled, "You're telling me this NOW???"

Livia looked at all the places in the room that she could look at so she didn't have to look at him. She shifted her eyes out the window, past his head. There was another building across the street. The windows were dark—she couldn't see the people inside.

"Why didn't you tell me?!" Jeffrey yelled. "Look at me!!"

Livia knew why she had not told him.

"I'm sorry," she said. She began to cry and he held her. She put her face in his chest.

"I'm sorry," she said, and she was. She knew she was a disappointment. She had always known this. Now she would be worse: she would be the reason for them to not go on.

"I can't do it," she said, wiping her mascara with her hands.

He took her away from his chest. She watched him look at her. He looked like he might cry too.

He wiped her eyes.

"But Liv, I thought we agreed that we both wanted a family," he said.

They had not talked about it much since they had been married. She never brought it up, and although sometimes he would make comments about babies, she just ignored him and changed the subject.

Livia looked at his sad face. She loved him then. She let him kiss her forehead, hold her, push her hair behind her ears. She had the feeling of fully surrendering to him. She could not let this go.

"I can," she said suddenly, smiling. "I can do it. You're right."

Jeffrey smiled back, then hugged her tightly.

Still, it took years until Abby finally came.

18.

Headie lies in the hallway that leads from the living room–kitchen area to the bedrooms. She has left two pillows there all day. She has heard that there are mites in pillows and in mattresses, but if she cannot see them, what is she supposed to do?

The two pillows are much smaller than a real bed: there will be fewer mites with less space for them to fill. But the ants . . . it makes her tired to think of it.

Headie used to think how strange it was that her own parents slept in separate beds. She remembers when she was a child how one of her friends told her that parents did that so that they didn't have more children.

In her second marriage, to Allen, Headie became a part of a two-bed couple. She did not want to be, and would have slept with her husband forever. She would have held him while he was dying. She would have stayed awake to pet his bald head.

But Allen had become uncomfortable. He said that he couldn't sleep anymore. So they bought two beds and pushed them next to each other. She tucked the sheets and blankets into each separate bed, but at night she would lie above the covers, rolling over to his side, ending up on his bed in the morning.

Her second marriage had been different from her first in many ways. She did not marry Gene for love and she did not marry him for comfort, at least not the comfort that left you fat and warm in a bed next to someone else who was fat and warm.

When Headie first married, she lay in her bed and waited for Gene to flop his arm over her in his sleep (he was a toss-and-turner). Then she focused on the arm, on the fingers that twitched like he was playing an instrument, and thought about what she had to do the next day.

It was not so much that she did not love him, it was that he would never love her. There was no point in loving someone who would never complete the love. It was like half a heart-shaped cookie. It was ridiculous.

Headie married after her father re-married. You couldn't stay in your father's house when someone else was there to do the things you used to, and you couldn't marry your father either.

You could live with a man who was kind. All you had to do was be a wife and take care of the house. You could do more or less what you did for your father, except the things that you did only with your husband.

Headie looks at the ceiling. It has been nice having the computer plugged in—she doesn't have to worry about getting up to answer calls. Now it is up to her when she wants to move. This is one of the things she loves about email: it will wait for her.

Still, there are other things to do. There are things to organize. There are dancers in the corners of her eyes.

Headie elbows herself on the ground, low like an army man, into the bathroom. She reaches up to the toilet bowl, then grabs the end of the sink. It is less that her legs are going, and more that she is just tired. This makes her feel better; all she needs is rest.

Once on the toilet, she pees and leans forward to open the bathroom cabinet on the wall across from her.

Everything is neat in the cabinet—the towels have all been washed and stacked, and all the medicines are in rows—some old, some new. From where she sits she cannot read the dates. The old ones have dark blue faded typing on them. The words are the color of bruises.

Headie squints. There are many toothbrushes, some used, some still in packages, lined up on the bottom shelf. There are different kinds of soaps: ones she picked up from hotels, a few special colored ones that Livia got her for her bath. The shelves are deep, and Headie cannot see past the first row of toiletries. It is time to clean.

Headie pushes herself off the toilet, forward, and in one quick motion sweeps her hands inside the shelves. She swipes everything out of the cabinet and holds on to the wall as the contents fall to the floor.

On the pink rug there are Q-tips, half-opened shampoo bottles, pieces of paper from soap bars and lotions she had forgotten about, which are yellow because they are old.

Headie slinks down to the floor, her back to the wall, and pulls up her underwear. The rug is small and now there is dirt in it. Whenever she tries to vacuum the rug it gets stuck to the nozzle. When she vacuums she has to stand on both ends of it, as if she is playing golf, and suction between them.

Headie rolls back over, her body on the tile floor, her hands raking through the stuff. She finds old makeup (a pink lipstick, an eye pencil) and barrettes that someone once must have left. She even finds two tampons (probably from Livia) and a small purple pad of paper.

Headie turns things over, picks them up and smells them while on her stomach, on the floor. She lines up the toothbrushes, the soaps, and the lotions, each on a separate part of the rug.

She has always been a good cleaner. She had to be: her mother died when she was young. She had to clean for her father. Her older sister was more social, and then got married and left. Her sister died young too.

When Headie finally left her father's house, she took her mother's old blanket, her gray and blue suits, and all of her shoes. She wore a skirt and blouse with a white jacket.

She took a train to her sister Naomi's house and watched from the window as the black smoke from the coal pits reached for the sky and then disappeared. She could see the shiny coal mines, huge ditches in the earth. The train ride was less than an hour, but the motion made her fall asleep.

Naomi picked her up at the station in a shiny new blue car. Her sister had aged in the years since she'd left home; she looked older than when Headie had seen her just months ago. Her husband, David, was nice enough, but Naomi had told her that after they got married he could get angry—he didn't hit her or anything, but he was sometimes irritable, sometimes mean.

Naomi wore drab clothes and thick leather shoes. The car was too fancy for her—it looked like she was driving it by mistake.

"You better stay out of David's way. I'm telling you, it's already a struggle with just Gene there," Naomi said after kissing her quickly and putting her bags in the trunk. "All day Gene goes to the hospital, and all day David goes to work, and they get home at the same time and the house is too small. David wants Gene out but I keep convincing him to let him stay."

"Why doesn't he want him there?" Headie asked.

"Because he thinks he's a wimp. You know David, he doesn't like weakness."

Gene: David's sad brother. He stuttered, and worse, his fiancée, Lilac, had gotten into a bad car accident. He had been staying with Naomi and David—he could not be alone. Lilac was in a bad way.

Headie thought of Gene's stutter, and his awkward neck. David was strong and tall. They did not look like siblings.

"Well, maybe it will be better with me here," Headie said, looking out at the town that would soon be her home. "I can help you, you know. I'll help you clean and cook, and I'll start applying for jobs tomorrow. It will be fine."

When they got to the house, Gene was moving his things out of the guest room so that Headie could move in. He would sleep in the den now, on a pullout couch.

Headie and Naomi lugged her two suitcases inside.
"You could have helped," Naomi said to Gene as he
plugged his alarm clock in next to the couch. Headie
watched as he placed a picture of Lilac next to it on the
end table. She was wearing a tight sweater on a beach,
her hand above her eyes. It was hard to see her, the way
the picture was taken. Someone forgot you weren't supposed to face a camera toward the sun.

"S-s-sorry," Gene stuttered, looking down at his big
feet. He was older than Headie by a year or so, but he
gave off the the impression of being a child.

Headie and Gene had met a number of times at
family gatherings, although she had mostly spoken to
Lilac. Lilac was always polite and sweet, but she was the
kind of woman who Headie couldn't tell what she was
thinking. Or if she was thinking at all.

At Naomi's wedding Headie did not have a date.
She had to walk down the aisle at the synagogue arm-
in-arm with Gene.

At the reception, Headie sat at the table with Gene
and Lilac. Lilac had blondish hair and a small nose but
she was not attractive (her eyes were too close together,
her teeth stuck out). Headie watched Gene rub the back
of her neck with his thumb, back and forth.

Then the music began playing. Lilac was wearing a
purple dress (of course), and when the first fast song
came on she smiled and took Gene's hand. Together
they skipped to the dance floor, and soon everyone sur-
rounded them as Gene held Lilac up, spun her around,
pulled her through his legs and picked her up again.
Everyone clapped, and Headie stood outside the circle

on her tiptoes so she could see. Lilac's hair fell down and small light curls appeared around her ears. It was like she became pretty because she was having so much fun and didn't care. Or because Gene thought so. Or because facing him, moving fast to the music, watching herself in her fiancé's eyes, it had become clear to her. In turn, she was pretty to everyone watching.

Lilac was flushed, and Gene was sweating. Watching them made Headie wish for many things.

In Naomi's house, Gene waved to Headie. She remembered what Naomi had told her about Gene not being drafted because of his flat feet. His feet had to stay home so that the girls that were left had a dancing partner, Headie thought.

Gene was holding a small brass-looking rocking horse in his hand that he put on the end table next to the clock and the photo. Headie felt too embarrassed for him to ask what it was.

In the guest room, Headie hung up her suits and lined up her shoes. Naomi stood in the doorway.

"Here's your towels. You're responsible for washing your own linens and cleaning your room. I feel like I'm running a boarding house!" Naomi said, blowing air up to her bangs.

"I will," Headie said. "I won't bother you."

Headie looked around the room and wondered how it could be arranged differently, what she would have to move. She wondered if, by the time she had the baby, she would be moved out. She was more than two months pregnant, and the room was too small to fit a crib.

From: abbyschecter15@yahoo.com
To: headragoldstein@aol.com

Dear Bubbe—

I am learning French, English, Social Studies II, Biology, Gym, and Chorus (that is my schedule).

Things are good. Friday is the Pep Rally and the Homecoming game.

I am making a decoy duck in tech class. When I'm done do you want it? It is made out of wood. I can send it to you.

How is Aunt Millie? Are you doing well? Have you explored the Internet more or are you still only sending email?

Love,

Abby

From: headragoldstein@aol.com
To: abbyschecter15@yahoo.com

ABBY I DO NOT NEED A DUCK. MILLIE FELL ON THE ICE BUT WHEN SHE IS BETTER SHWILL HELP ME MAYBE GET ON THE INTERNET I DONT CARE I WRITE TO YOU AND YOUR FATHER AND YOURMOTHER. PLEASE DONT SEND THE DUCK LOVE YOUR BUBBE

19.

The first day of Driver's Ed Abby and Alec and another girl, Carlie Blake, sit on the curb of the school parking lot waiting for Mr. Sims.

Abby looks at her knee next to Alec's (he is sitting between her and Carlie). It seems too close.

"Is your dad really teaching us?" Carlie asks.

"Yup," he says, nodding his head as if he is saying hello to someone in the halls. He has not spoken to Abby, or slammed her locker, since he called her ugly.

"Oh," Carlie says. She is a jock, but pretty in a way, and not someone anyone would make fun of. She has big shoulders—swimmer's shoulders—even though she plays field hockey and basketball.

Abby says nothing. She reaches in her pocket and feels the outline of her pack of cigarettes beneath the liner in her army jacket.

In her other pocket she feels bits of loose tobacco.

Just yesterday Abby watched Chess's profile in the driver's seat of his car and fingered the same bits. She had been walking across the parking lot to the woods to go home when a horn honked behind her.

"Want a ride?" Chess asked from the high seat of his Jeep.

Abby got in and Chess drove out of the parking lot, out onto the road, then past her driveway.

"Wait," she said.

He didn't look at her. He just smirked.

"There's pot in the glove compartment," he said.

Just yesterday, in Chess's car, she mixed her tobacco with his pot and rolled a joint. Chess told Abby to take the wheel for a second while he lit it. She steered the car halfway around a bend on a small, empty road. Then he took the wheel back from her, his palms hitting her knuckles, and drove.

Abby watches Alec out of the corner of her eye. He does not look at her, just out to the road where his father will drive into the parking lot. Abby wonders what kind of father would have Alec as a son.

It makes her think: what if her mother had to teach Driver's Ed? She tries to see her mother from someone else's point of view, but it's hard. She can see her walking from one room to the next, heavy-footed, looking at the floor. She can see her profile in the front seat of their car, driving her when it is Jorgen's day off.

If her mother had to teach Driver's Ed she would probably quit after the first class. She would probably get frustrated and leave, crying and hating someone she had just met.

Abby wishes Chess could teach her Driver's Ed. Just yesterday, as they passed the parking lot near the park on their way into town, Abby asked if she could drive.

"You know how?" he asked.

The last time she had "driven" she had been young enough to sit on her father's lap and turn the wheel.

"Yup!" she said.

"Next time, maybe," he said, smirking, shifting, driving. He turned in to the park near town, and parked the car in the lot. He got out without saying anything, and she followed him as he walked past the jungle gym and the sandbox, into the woods.

There was a big rock with graffiti on it that she could tell he had been to before.

"How do you know where all this stuff is?" she asked, sitting on the rock next to him, taking out her cigarettes.

"I don't know . . . guys on the team . . . I just moved here in the summer," he said, as if she hadn't noticed.

"I know," she said, wishing she hadn't. "Why?"

She watched him light a cigarette, cupping and lighting it with the same hand. She looked at his fingernails: they looked bit.

"My mom," he said. "She wanted to move out of the city. They're divorced. My dad still lives there."

Abby looked at his red puffy vest and plaid shirt and wondered which parent bought his clothes for him. What kind of parents had a boy that looked like him? She could imagine a father, but not a mother. His father would look just like him.

Abby is cold outside the gym. She closes her jacket around her without zipping it up. She looks quickly over at Alec. She wants to ask him where his father is. Isn't he out of work? Can't he be on time?

She would not have said this before the night on the lawn, and she does not say it now. Perhaps on the outside she seems the same to him.

"Yo Sims!" she hears Chess's sweet, deep voice from behind her. He is at the head of the pack of football players running out of the gym for practice, dressed in pads and sweats. He runs over to where they are sitting on the curb. Alec stands and they do the boy hand thing where they touch shoulders after shaking a certain way.

"What's up?" Alec says.

"You have practice?" Carlie says to him.

Abby smiles and says nothing. She wonders if Chess ever fucked Carlie.

"Hey," Chess says to Abby. He half smiles.

"We're waiting for Alec's dad," Abby says, then feels bad when she sees Alec blush.

"It's cold," Chess says. "You ready for tomorrow?"

He winks at her. They have a secret.

Because Carlie is there, no one says anything. The bottle of lemon-flavored vodka is sleeping beneath her bed, turned sideways, on its back, just waiting. The bottle is silent, unscented and sealed.

"Good luck tomorrow," Carlie says to Chess.

"Yeah," says Chess, slapping Alec on the shoulder. "You too," he says, looking at Abby, then walks away onto the field.

Yesterday, at the park on the rock, Chess looked at her sideways with those same eyes.

"Are your parents divorced?" he asked.

She wondered if it would be OK if she kept lighting cigarettes, one after another, and they could just stay there until dark, or forever.

"No," she said. "But they're weird."

Chess laughed. He looked so good smoking. She wanted to know who gave him his first cigarette. She tried to imagine him as a child.

She tried to imagine him being in a situation that he could not smile his way out of.

"Yeah," Chess said. "Tell me about it."

A car beeps behind them and Mr. Sims gets out of the car and waves. He is shorter than Alec, and smaller, and wearing a suit. He has red hair and freckled hands.

"Hey guys," he says to the three of them, as if Alec is not his son, or else Carlie and Abby are. "You ready to go?"

Carlie volunteers to go first, and Alec and Abby sit next to each other in the back seat. As soon as Carlie makes her first turn in the parking lot, Mr. Sims presses down on the passenger seat break.

Abby and Alec lurch forward in their seat belts.

"Now, Carlie," Mr. Sims says. "What did I say about checking the rearview first?"

Yesterday, Chess told her on the rock, "They're not as weird as mine."

Abby laughed, then said, "My mom tried to kill herself."

It sounded weird, saying it. It escaped her mouth, and now it was too late. What if Chess was tricking her? What if Jenna was behind the rock or in the woods, waiting to pop out and surprise her? She had never said those words before; she had never even written them.

Chess nodded and didn't say anything. He didn't even look surprised. He was silent for a minute. No one popped out from behind the rock. Abby's heart began to beat a bit slower. She breathed deep; it felt good.

It was silent and there was the wind. Then Chess said, "My mom has a girlfriend."

At first Abby thought she'd heard wrong.

"You mean . . ." she said.

Chess nodded. A leaf blew behind him from a tree to the ground.

"They live together?" she asked.

"Yup," he said, "but don't tell Jenna or anyone. OK?" He turned and looked at her. He put his hand on her face, flat on her cheek. He looked sad, maybe, but then smiled, taking his hand away.

Abby would never tell a soul.

After they left the park he drove them through town. When he drove fast it was hard to hear anything, so she was quiet.

He put on music she didn't know and she listened while he sang along to it. She wished she knew the songs so she could play them later, alone in her room, when she got home.

In the car, now, Abby wants to look over at Alec to see what his expression is. She wonders if he has the type of family where he can actually roll his eyes at what his parents say, or whether has to keep his eyes still and roll them inside his head where no one can see them.

Abby looks at Mr. Sims's white-knuckled hands on the dash in the passenger seat. He turns sideways, and looks at her and smiles.

"Better not get too comfortable," he says to Abby. "Next time you're up!"

20.

Once they are in bed, Livia tells Jeffrey that she has plans for tomorrow night.

"What do you mean?" he asks, turning his body to face her.

Usually Jeffrey likes to go out to eat or to a movie on weekend nights. Sometimes they have to go out with his partners and their wives, Anne and Jenny, both dyed blondes. Anne is a real estate agent; Jenny is a stay-at-home mom. They are not only married to matching lawyers, they are also best friends.

When they go out, Livia tries to make small talk, pushing the restaurant food on her plate around and around. She drinks wine and tries to listen. Anne and Jenny have to fill her in on the background of whatever they are talking about (explaining that so–and–so is one of their children's friends' mothers who is such a snob and belongs/does not belong to the Club, and has a devil of a child or a lovely one, etc.).

In the past Livia sometimes talked about her master's. Sometimes she brings up a book that she knows they haven't read. It bothers her that no matter what she talks about, every time she talks, she can feel Jeffrey listening to her. Even while he is in another conversation, Jeffrey monitors her. It makes her want to flip the table over. Or worse, say something about their marriage.

"I have a late meeting at Simone's house. I expect I'll be back after nine-thirty or so," Livia says, washing down her Klonopin with water so she can sleep.

"I wish you had told me," Jeffrey says, opening his book, *The Tipping Point*.

It always surprises Livia that he wanted to do anything with her; she mostly feels like a burden to him. His biggest emotion toward her seems to be worry. Worrying about something she'll say, or worse, do.

But it has been years since Jeffrey had to worry. Years since things had been that bad. If she'd known that he would never get over it, maybe she wouldn't have done it. Maybe she would have just stayed in bed like she does so often now, and slept it off.

But years ago, when Abby was only eight, she did not go back to sleep.

They didn't have an au pair then, just a babysitter who came in the afternoons. In the morning it was Livia's job to get Abby ready for school.

One morning, Livia opened her eyes and saw Jeffrey tying his tie on the other side of the room. She didn't want him to know she was awake.

"Caught you," he said, walking over and leaning down to kiss her forehead, his tie dangling in her eyes.

"Leave me alone," she said.

"You only have ten minutes. Come have some coffee with me."

"No," Livia said, turning over, hoping to get back to sleep quickly.

Jeffrey kissed her cheek, then left and closed the door behind him. Livia reached between her legs.

That morning she thought about sex—she felt horny for some reason. It felt like it had been a long time since she masturbated. She thought of her old sex drive; for years it was what drove her. In her twenties she hardly ate because she wanted sex; she could think of little else. Back then she was always searching for someone to keep up with her.

Jeffrey kept up with her for a while in the beginning. But then she began thinking of other men. She found herself wanting to masturbate more than make love. Then, after Abby, that stopped too.

With her hands between her thighs, still in bed, lying sideways, Livia thought about what to do next. She realized she did not want to masturbate (suddenly the thought seemed terribly depressing—she couldn't get out of her head how she would feel afterward). She thought about food.

She thought about the kitchen, what was in it, what she could make, but she wasn't hungry.

There were diet corn muffins (she loved corn muffins) that she had eaten in the night. She felt them, heavy in her stomach. No, she did not want to eat.

She thought about other things: sex, work, a cigarette. She thought about the book she was reading. She thought about sleeping more, but she was awake.

She thought about traveling and jewels and houses she would have loved to buy. She thought about swimming.

And then she thought about dreams.

At that time, before she used a computer, she wrote her dreams down on paper in the morning. She had a black leather notebook that she kept next to her bed. Usually it was the first thing she did, without even sitting up, just reached sideways and wrote.

She realized, then, what was different, why nothing could move her: she could not remember her dream from the night before. It was the first time she could remember not remembering.

Usually Livia kept her dreams with her for at least the beginning of the day. The rest of her day was often filled with tiny bits of déjà vu, or flashbacks, when she was driving or eating, to something that had happened while she slept.

She thought about her dream from two nights before where she had been walking behind a woman in the street with an obscenely wide ass. But she could not get last night's dream in her head.

Abby knocked on the door while she was thinking.

"What?" she asked, loud enough for her to hear through the wall.

"I have to go to school," her little voice said.

Livia did not turn to see her daughter come in the room.

"Can you get yourself breakfast? I'm really not feeling well," she told her.

"Should I call Daddy?" Abby asked.

"No, just get on the bus. I'll be OK."

She lay in bed, listening to the soft sounds of Abby making her way in the kitchen, her small sneakers walking lightly on the tiles.

She heard a bowl or a mug fall, but Abby didn't call her name, and Livia didn't get up to see what was wrong. She heard Abby go into the bathroom, flush, run the sink water, and finally open the door to leave.

When she heard the front door screen slam, Livia went back to trying to remember. She was hoping to fall back asleep, like she often did, after taking a pill to help her relax.

She closed her eyes. She did not have anything to do until the babysitter came. Then she would have to think of somewhere to go. Or she could say she was working in her bedroom and just eat or sleep more.

In the dream two nights ago, the woman with the fat ass would not turn around. You could see each pocket of fat, even though her pants were loose.

Livia remembered feeling glad that she was not as fat as the woman in the pants.

But last night. What was it? She had one small flash, something in a forest . . . but then nothing. Nothing. She would not get up—she couldn't move—until she remembered her dream.

Because if Livia could not remember her dreams, if she was becoming someone who had no sense of her internal life, if she was not special and was only a woman who no longer wanted sex from her husband—if she could not remember her dreams and had no other distractions left, if she could not remember her dreams and did not have a career, then what was it that she was doing? Where was her soul?

And if this was the truth, if the truth was that she was empty, then what?

She wished she could remember her dream.

Livia leaned over and took a pill, washing it down with the soda she had next to her bed from the night before. She had to take two pills to actually go to sleep, so after swallowing one she took another.

She looked up at the ceiling. There was a cobweb. The cleaning woman had not gotten it.

She closed her eyes and began to cry. She held herself, turned sideways, and tried to remember what it felt like the day before when Abby had brought home her artwork and they had hung it, together, on the corkboard at the art station she had made.

She wished she hadn't eaten those fucking corn muffins.

She could not stop crying; she could not remember feeling this way since college, since the time after sophomore year when she came home to her childhood bed on summer break. It was as if the spell of the year—all the activities and all the learning—suddenly stopped. Back with her parents, she began to feel the opposite of how she had felt at school.

A month after coming home from college she could not get out of bed; she could not stop crying. She could not even go back to school that fall. She took too much of her mother's Valium but made herself throw it up.

She took classes at the community college and her parents took her to a psychiatrist who hardly said anything. She went for a few sessions, and eventually distracted herself again. The following semester she was able to go back to school.

But that day, when Abby was eight, she felt the pills relieve her of this feeling for a moment, which made her breathing slow, which made her reach again for the bottle and take two more.

What had she dreamed?

She had never told Jeffrey about the semester off from college. Jeffrey had not seen her like this; he would never have married her.

Jeffrey had married her and she had become his wife. She kept her dreams to herself. Now she had none to keep.

Livia reached again and washed the rest of the pills in the bottle down with soda. She didn't think about what would happen if it didn't work. She didn't think about how the babysitter would come, find the front door unlocked with her nowhere in sight, her bedroom door closed with no one answering. She didn't think how, eventually, after knocking and knocking, the babysitter would open the door and find her, turned sideways, unwakeable, with barely a pulse. She didn't think how she would be carried from the house, outside into the air, hardly breathing, all the way to the hospital, where her daughter would see her, almost dead. She didn't imagine any of this until much later, after she woke up and her husband was there with a new look on his face.

At first she couldn't recognize the face on her husband: it was concerned, worried, scared. Eventually, when it didn't leave, she realized it was none of those. This new face was not a mask, was not temporary. It was a face that said that as much as I try, as much as I want to, as much as I care, I can truly, regrettably, no longer trust you.

It is the face Livia has woken up to each morning since. It is a reminder, just like some mornings when she cannot remember her dreams.

21.

In the bathroom Headie peers into a small powder case that came down from the shelf. There is no more powder, just a powdery mirror that she blows the dust from. She looks at her reflection, sitting up now, her back against the bathroom wall, and wonders if she appears the same to other people as she does to herself.

In pictures Headie always looks one way, but when she talks she knows she looks another. Sometimes, when she doesn't smile, she likes the way she looks better. She didn't appreciate her youth when she had it, she thinks, staring at her wrinkled lips in the compact.

The last time Headie went to the beauty salon she asked for a redder red (Millie had suggested it), so they had dyed her hair darker, blowing it out to cover her balding spots and the flatness in the back, like they did every week. Now her hair ("Fireside Chestnut") was flat on her scalp.

On her palms her skin is like wax. She does not have the smell she used to have when she was younger, a smell she had always liked. She holds the mirror away from her so she can see her neck and chest. She holds it down so she can see her belly.

She has always been glad she didn't have a cesarean like Naomi had. When Naomi gained weight, her stomach looked like a Wonder Bread loaf with that crack—"the butter"—sewn up sideways. Headie always thought that Naomi had had a cesarean because her daughter, Julia, had been so big. But Julia had turned out much smaller than it had seemed she would at first. Eventually Julia ended up fat, then bulimic, then a drug addict. She lives in California now and calls Headie sometimes, sounding strange and high.

Julia came out only a few weeks after Jeffrey. Jeffrey was jaundiced, and smaller, and Headie knew how he must have felt. Julia had hair, and a few months later Naomi pierced her ears. When Headie and Jeffrey were alone she would whisper to him, telling him things she didn't tell anyone.

Headie had always tried to make him feel strong. When he grew tall and filled out, she was glad. His father was tall, too.

Headie puts the mirror down and leans back to look at the ceiling. The white light fixture looks as if it has tiny dots on it. There is a flower shape in the middle. She has never noticed that before.

She looks down again into her lap, and then they are back, dancing. It is Allen this time, dancing with another woman. Allen is leading her quickly; the woman cannot keep up. He twirls her fast and it makes Headie dizzy. She feels badly for the woman whom Allen will not let go of.

Headie was already almost twenty-five at Allen's first wedding. She was involved in the synagogue, was part of the Sisterhood, and attended most of the ceremonies. She squeezed her hands together as his bride came down the aisle, looking at the floor and blushing.

She looked like she was scared to be there, or like she was there against her will, her gentile parents on either side of her, walking her slowly.

The bride's blonde hair was pulled back tightly, and she did not have a hint on her of what she would become. A year later, Headie walked in on her in the bathroom at the synagogue drinking from a flask. When Headie saw her on the street she would try to focus only on her feet, which were always nice and manicured in the summer. Her feet did not age over the years the way the rest of her did.

"He has affairs," Naomi said on the phone only a few months later. Headie had just told her what his wife was wearing that day in synagogue.

"How do you know?" Headie asked, twisting the phone cord in her father's house.

Naomi was three years older, married, and talked like she knew everything.

"Trust me," she said, laughing.

Almost a year and a half after his wedding, two months and two days after he had lifted her onto him in the store, and the day before she was to move in with her sister, Headie got up the nerve to walk by his office. In gold, on the office door, it said "Goldstein and Goldstein." She always thought it was strange that business people did that. Why not say Goldstein's? The Two Goldsteins? The Amazing Goldsteins!

Headie saw her reflection in the glass that blocked the office with a sheer curtain. She wore a plaid jacket, brown shoes, and a matching brown handbag in case he saw her walking by. She tried to ignore her own face in the window and look through the curtains but she could not focus—she was in the way.

Headie remembered how he had held her thighs, rubbing his thumbs back and forth over them and making marks on her skin.

On her last day of work, before she moved in with Naomi, she walked and looked down, thinking how, soon, when her stomach got bigger, she wouldn't even be able to see her shoes.

Then she heard his voice and looked up, just as he was halfway out the door, shaking another man's hand. She walked toward the hand as it waved its five fingers and the man got in the car. Then she was in front of the hand that had once touched her, and she wondered what hands would remember if they had a memory, if they had a brain. If they were their very own, his hands, and not controlled by him, perhaps they would have loved her; she had been good to them.

He stepped out when he saw her and closed the door behind him.

"Hi there," he said in his big voice, lighting a cigarette.

How strange it was to be standing next to him as if nothing had happened. It seemed ridiculous, the way they were apart now, after they had already been so together. How could they stand that way?

"I'm moving to my sister's in Wilkesboro," Headie said.

"Well that sounds nice," he said, one arm crossed on his chest, not looking at her but past her, around her, over her head.

Headie thought about telling him the secret that would crack him, right there in the street: she held the beginning of the tiniest blue-eyed baby inside her.

She looked up at him. He was smiling at the world and the sky and everyone in town but her. She could not catch his eye. She did not say anything.

She wondered how many women there were who knew him like she did.

"Well then," Allen said, putting out his cigarette in the outside ashtray, then holding the Goldstein and Goldstein door like he was letting someone out or helping someone in. "Good luck."

Allen winked one blue eye at her, half smiled, and went inside. She turned away as the door closed, then began walking, thinking of every step she made from where they had stood and how she was still at a spot where she could turn around and change something. The air was still there—she could do it—but then some more steps, more steps, and she realized she couldn't.

Not now now now.

Not now.

22.

Livia drives toward the Neck, all her evidence on the seat beside her. It is getting dark, and she drives onto the Causeway, the sun going down on her left. Livia turns into Simone's pebble driveway.

She has been up since the morning, has not had a nap, not all day. All day she has been in bed, but not asleep. She has been on the Internet instead. She has been studying; now she is ready. She is set to talk about color.

All day she has been researching color, looking for as many Web sites as possible that support her initial idea: match the hues with the nature.

Now she has it. Color printouts, text, samples, and the multiple books (as well as some horrible mauve just in case).

The windows on the first floor of Simone's house glow a homey yellow. There is a set of planters on either side of the front door. New. She did not know they wanted planters.

Livia gets out of the car and goes around the other side to get all of her samples. Her arms are full when she rings the doorbell, and when Simone answers she laughs and reaches out her hands to help her.

"Wow!" Simone says, walking barefoot, in light khaki pants and a blue T-shirt, into the sunroom.

Livia remembers and takes off her shoes, puts them next to some small, white sneakers that were not there last time.

She follows Simone, puts the books down on the floor next to the couch, and sits.

"Livia's here, hon," Simone calls up the stairs, then goes into the kitchen and yells out, "Is white wine OK?"

Livia realizes she left the bottles of red she brought in the car. She thinks about saying something, but doesn't. Red is not for this occasion, apparently. She was wrong.

She sits and looks out the window. There are no lights on in the backyard, the sun is setting orange. She hears footsteps coming down the stairs.

"I'm coming," says a singsongy feminine voice.

Both women enter the room at the same time: Simone comes from the kitchen, and Gail from the front hall. Gail appears, all blonde curly hair knotted through itself, with tendrils coming down at the sides. She is wearing white shorts and a white shirt that cover yet highlight her toned and tanned body. Gail reaches out her hand and smiles big white teeth.

"It's so good to finally meet you!" she says, shaking Livia's hand.

The two women sit across from Livia on ugly matching chairs that she does not remember being there last time (she will have those re-covered soon). Simone hands each of them a glass and pours wine into them while Gail talks.

"I've heard so much about you!" Gail says, crossing her legs. Livia wonders what Gail looks like when she is going to work, whether she ties those curls up or slicks them back, to be taken more seriously.

Looking at both of them across from her, Livia wonders, which one is the man?

Gail looks flushed, like she has just come from playing tennis somewhere glamorous, or else has just had an orgasm.

"And I you," Livia says, lifting her glass, almost saying "*L'chaim*" but remembering, stopping herself, saying "Cheers!"

"I just love your house. I'm so excited to be working on it!" Livia says. She can hear her own voice, out of her, across the room. It does not sound like her. She sounds like her mother.

Her mother who smoked a cigarette after each meal and had themed parties. Her mother, who prided herself on being a hostess, who made (or had someone make) fondue.

Her mother, who once told her that all men cheated.

Livia wonders what her mother would do. Should she launch right into her spiel (she has practiced, she is anxious) or else get to know Gail, calm down, the way Jeffrey always tells her.

She takes a breath. This is important.

"The light in here is breathtaking," Livia says, taking a sip from her glass.

Gail looks younger than Simone. If Simone does not look like a typical lesbian, Gail is the straightest-looking lesbian in the world. She is beautiful.

Livia takes another sip and brushes her hair back from her face so that it falls forward. She looks sexier this way, Jeffrey says.

Livia takes another sip and tries to remember what she thought Gail would look like. She remembers short dark hair, pretty maybe, but not this. Nothing like this. Not sun-kissed with apple cheeks, blue eyes, and smooth skin. Not barefoot with a thin gold ankle bracelet and the air of someone from nowhere near here, from California or Sweden. That's it: she looks like an au pair. She looks like she was paid to come here. Why else, Livia thinks, would she have a partner instead of a man?

"So, you've lived in the area for a long time?" Gail asks.

"Well, I've been here four years now. We're from Philadelphia," she says, glad to be asked.

"It's great here," Gail says, looking out the back window toward the boat and the dusk. "We're so happy to have found it," she says, not looking at Simone while saying "we."

"Looks like you brought a lot to show us," Simone says, taking a quick sip, then getting up and reaching for a book. "May I?" she asks.

"Oh, of course," Livia says. "Actually, let me show you some of my ideas."

"Look!" Gail says, suddenly. Livia follows Gail's pointed finger to the bay where a full pink moon is rising, the sky still not-yet-night.

"It's gorgeous," Simone says.

"Yes," Livia agrees.

She wishes her own house were on the bay. Instead it is on a street, set back, with land, but no swimming pool (yet!). No view.

Perhaps when her business gets bigger they could move. Sometimes Livia thinks they could move now if Jeffrey were interested. But Jeffrey is not interested, so she does not bring it up. Jeffrey is always fine with doing nothing.

"It's so nice to be near the water," Gail says.

Livia watches as Gail stands and walks toward the window. She can't imagine that this woman ever had a baby. Her leg muscles are defined. Probably a runner.

She looks over at Simone who she sees is watching Gail too. As usual, frustratingly, she wonders what goes on behind closed doors. When she used to talk more to Jeffrey about these things, she would speculate, and try to get him to speculate with her.

She would ask about his partners. Their wives. Do you think they have affairs? she would ask. He got annoyed, told her that men didn't talk to each other that way, that he wouldn't know, it was business.

Livia wonders if Gail and Simone stay up late, eating popcorn and gossiping. Perhaps they tell each other their dreams.

Gail turns around and turns on the light next to the door. All her tiny curls turn white.

"So, show us your portfolio," she says, sitting back down across from Livia.

Livia puts her glass down, carefully, next to her on the table. She tries not to shake.

"Oh, no," she says. She can feel herself blush. "I forgot to bring it. I didn't realize . . ."

"Oh, that's OK," Simone says. "Next time."

"Sure," Livia says. "I'm just updating it."

Livia looks over at Simone, who is smiling at her. She sees Simone differently today, more like a mom. Or weaker, maybe. Weak to a beautiful woman named Gail.

She wonders if Simone's impression of her would change if she met Jeffrey. Perhaps she would think she was weak, or spacey, or incompetent. Perhaps she would see her through Jeffrey's eyes.

There is no living room table in the living room, so Livia spreads out her books and samples on the floor. Gail comes down from the chair and sits Indian style, and Simone sits with her legs to the side next to her.

Livia sits with her legs to the side too (she is wearing a skirt) and turns the pages, feeling the teal fabrics, making Gail and Simone touch them the way the interior designer at the store had done with her when she had been getting advice. Livia says "lush."

"I like this," Gail says, pointing with her light manicured fingernail to a tannish-brown fabric opposite the page that Livia was showing them.

"Well, actually," Livia says, "I wanted to talk to you a little bit about my concept for your house. Since you have so many windows and so much light, and you have the water right there, I think the best way to play up the gorgeous natural beauty, to bring it inside, in a way, is to echo the colors from outside."

Gail smiles, looking out the window. The boat lights are beginning to glow.

"Yes, but don't we just look out the window for that? I mean, don't we want to feel like we are in a different space?"

Gail is not being mean when she says this—Livia knows this. She is honestly asking a question. She looks at Livia to respond.

"It's one way to go," Livia says. "But the idea would be to play up the outside, making it almost like a surreal version. I'm not sure that's the word, but what I mean is that instead of, say, the dull blue of the water, instead you would have colors like the teal blue, or even a darker aqua."

"Hmmm," Gail says.

"I like it," says Simone.

Livia looks into Gail's eyes, waiting for her to agree. They are light and not evil but hard to see clearly with the last ray of sun coming through on all of them.

23.

Headie wakes up on the bathroom floor, her head on the rug, her legs bent sideways, her toes against the bottom of the sink. The trashcan that she had begun to throw some of the cabinet contents out in has been turned over, and now the stuff is spilled everywhere again.

Just as well, Headie figures. She has not thrown it out for so long, maybe she should just keep all of it. It seems like too much of a decision.

There are no windows in the bathroom, and she does not know if it is day or night. She begins to pull herself forward on the floor. This goes smoothly on the bathroom tiles, reaching with her arms, then bending her elbows, her body like dead weight behind her. But when she reaches the carpet of the hallway her body no longer moves easily.

Still she slithers, using her hips as if they were small feet, one forward, then the other. She wonders if she is hungry. She misses the computer.

Once in the kitchen, she slides herself quickly again over the tile. She looks up at the windows—it is dark outside. She is glad she left the lights on—the last thing she wants is to stand and flick the switch. She reaches up, on her knees, holding on to the chair, and brings the computer to the floor.

She presses the button, lying on her stomach, the computer making its noise.

"You've got mail," it tells her. There are five baby envelopes, and she is glad.

To: headragoldstein@aol.com
From: millieschwartz@aol.com

Headie—
How are you? I promise to come over soon. I'm feeling much better. The kids are supposed to come up this weekend.
I don't feel well enough to drive to synagogue anyway. You understand.
Love,
Millie

To: headragoldstein@aol.com
From: abbyschecter15@yahoo.com

Hi Bubbe—
I did not send you the duck—don't worry.
I just started Driver's Ed. Don't worry, I'm careful. I can't wait to drive! I never understood the way people could drive and talk at the same time but now I can!
Tonight is the Pep Rally at school. It is for the big home-coming game. I don't really care about sports, but me and my friend Jenna are going.
Love,
Abby

To: headragoldstein@aol.com
From jwschecter@schecterglasspeters.com

Mom—
You HAVE to UNPLUG your computer and PLUG IN
your phone in order for you to get phone calls. PLEASE do
this. I'll call Millie if I can't get through later. You worry me.
Love,
Jeffrey

Jeffrey W. Schecter
Attorney at Law
Schecter, Glass and Peters Associates

To: headragoldstein@aol.com
From: millieschwartz@aol.com

Dear Headie,
Jeffrey called to tell me that you haven't plugged your
phone back in. Remember when I showed you? Just take out
the computer jack thing and put back the phone one.
I told him we've been emailing and not to worry and
about my fall. I don't think he's worried anymore but call me
after you do it.
Love, Millie

To: headragoldstein@aol.com
From: jwschecter@schecterglasspeters.com

Mom—

I spoke to Millie and she said that she showed you how to put the plug in. So you should do it, OK?

Millie told me about her fall. If you can't figure out how to plug the phone in, then email me and let me know. This is ridiculous!

Love,
Jeffrey

Jeffrey W. Schecter
Attorney at Law
Schecter, Glass and Peters Associates

Headie closes the computer and looks at the jack behind the chair. She looks up at her telephone on the wall. She is too tired to move.

Headie rolls over again. She does not want to look at the ceiling so she closes her eyes. She does not want to slither over to the jack so she doesn't. It is nice, she thinks, doing nothing.

She rolls her eyes back in her sockets just because it feels good. She has a strange thought: for so long she has had to see. She thinks that for the first time she doesn't want to, so she falls into the blackness and thinks of Jeffrey.

Worried Jeffrey. Perhaps she can send him her thoughts and tell him that she is fine. If she thinks hard enough, perhaps he will know she is just resting. Perhaps he will see her, suddenly, while he is in his office. A flash will come and she will appear, relaxed. He will see her and forgive her.

She had wanted to tell him for years. She thought about telling him after Gene died, but she did not. She did not tell him, either, when he went off to college. She did not tell him when she told Jeffrey and Livia that she was going to marry Allen.

If there were ever a time to tell him, and there had been many, Headie knew the time to do it was then. If only Livia hadn't been there with her big tearing eyes and her ripped jeans and sleeveless shirt, kneeling at Headie's legs with Jeffrey.

"Mom," she said. She called her "mom" now. "You can't! You just can't!"

They sat at her knees, begging her not to marry him. She wished they would at least sit down, or even stand above her and order her to stop.

Jeffrey and Livia were visiting from New York, and the night before Headie had had Allen over for dinner. He came in his suit.

"Hiya," he said, slapping Jeffrey on the back.

"Ladies," he said, kissing Livia's hand, then kissing Headie on the cheek.

Allen was still tall and big but the top of his head was shiny-bald now. He was still a powerful lawyer, and Headie knew she was lucky.

Allen sat down at the head of the table before he was invited, and asked Headie to take the soda and wine off the table and put it in the fridge. His wife had died three months before.

Headie loved him. She cleared the drinks, sat down, and looked at her two men.

Allen and Jeffrey looked alike. They both had blue eyes—Headie and Gene did not. Headie had heard once that a man went bald if his mother's father went bald, and her father had not. So Jeffrey, with his blue eyes and height and long legs and maybe the set of his jaw, would not go bald like his father.

Livia stared at Allen as he ate, not saying anything.

"So," Livia asked Allen, finally. "How was your day?"

Livia was antagonistic. At her house, with her parents, she was loud. Jeffrey had told Headie how her family was, how they fought, how once, before they were married, Livia had had a temper tantrum in front of him, lying down and banging her fists on the floor, until she got her way.

"Fine, fine," Allen said, wiping his mouth.

"Anything new at work?" Livia asked.

Headie got up to clear the salad plates. They had been on the table way too long.

"Some things," he said, chuckling, then looking back down at his food.

"Do you think I wouldn't understand them?" asked Livia, her face getting red, the little storm inside her about to break.

"Young lady," he said, pushing his chair back. "I'd rather not discuss my business when I am eating a dinner made by such a wonderful hostess."

Headie paused behind his chair, and he leaned the back of his bald head on her apron.

"Thank you," she said, patting his head, then making her way around the table, picking up more things.

"I'm going to get some more wine," Livia said and walked into the kitchen.

"Will you bring in enough for everyone else?" Allen called.

The next morning, Livia and Jeffrey sat before her.

"He is not going to be my stepfather. There is no way that I will bow down to him, Mom," Jeffrey said.

"His wife just died! Isn't that weird for you?" Livia asked.

"She had been sick," Headie said, "for a long time."

"Aunt Naomi said that she killed herself with alcohol."

"Aunt Naomi talks too much," Headie said, leaning back in the chair, then getting up to put on hot water for tea.

It was not the time to tell him.

24.

In the last bathroom stall in the empty girls' locker room, Abby unzips her backpack while Jenna sits on the toilet seat in her jeans and purple coat. She wears her purple hoop earrings to match because, she tells Abby, she will probably keep her coat on all night.

It is dark in the locker room but they can see; the last light of the day shines faintly through the high windows. They cannot turn on the lights—no one can know they are there.

Abby takes out the bottle from her backpack.

"Open it! I'm so excited!"

Abby is wearing the same lucky jeans she wore the night that Alec frenched her. They are the same jeans she wore when they were on the lawn and she told him to stop.

The lucky jeans give her a strange feeling. She does not know what she wants to be lucky for. She wonders if she needs to have some kind of wish to make it come true, or if luck is different—a surprise—that knows what you want before you do.

Abby twists off the top of the bottle and puts her nose up to it. She breathes in deep to see if she can smell the lemon, but she can't. The smell makes her gag.

"Hold your nose," Jenna says, and Abby does, then lifts the bottle and takes a large swallow. She hands Jenna the vodka and makes an ugly face.

"It's terrible," she says, the taste blooming inside her mouth now that she has stopped holding her nose.

Jenna takes the next swig.

"It's not that bad," she says.

Abby watches the way Jenna holds the bottle back. Abby does the same and gulps. She is worried she is not getting as much. She drinks more.

"I'm hot," Jenna says, taking off her coat. Abby takes hers off too and they both light cigarettes.

"Where did you go with Chess the other day?" Jenna asks, putting her hair back in a ponytail.

"How did you know?" Abby asks, looking away from her where the smoke is rising out of the stall, then taking the bottle and another big sip. Maybe she had been right. It was a trick. It makes her feel like crying.

"He told me you guys took a ride. Why? Was it a secret?" Jenna says.

"No," Abby says, thinking of her secret. It couldn't have been a trick. Why would he tell her about his mom if it weren't true? Having a lesbian mom was worse than having a dead one.

"Well, don't you think he's hot?" Jenna says.

Abby laughs. "Yes." She thinks of his hand, flat and cool and steady on her cheek.

"You should fuck him," Jenna says, standing up and stomping her cigarette butt into the tile floor instead of flushing it in the toilet.

"Shut up," Abby says, taking another swig. There is no way, she decides, that he told Jenna. Abby holds the secret. She feels drunk but she knows she will never tell.

It feels darker suddenly without the glow from Jenna's cigarette. Abby can hear yelling outside: Pep Rally.

She takes two sips. Jenna takes one, and Abby takes another. Just to be sure she is feeling it.

"Seriously," Jenna says. "Didn't I teach you anything?" Jenna laughs.

Abby laughs too, following Jenna out of the stall, thinking of Jenna teaching her something. She feels lightheaded. She does not feel angry. She remembers Jenna and Jorgen but she can't remember the way she usually does. She can't get her head to stay in one place.

"I am really drunk," she says, sitting down on one of the locker room benches.

"Yeah, so you should fuck him," Jenna says, following Abby.

Abby laughs again and looks at Jenna. She waits for Jenna's face to crack, to show a smile. But it doesn't. She puts her purple jacket back on. Abby is confused.

"Let's go," Jenna says, and walks toward the door.

Abby takes a big swig.

Jenna takes one too, and then gives her back the bottle. Abby holds her nose and drinks. The bottle is lighter. She gulps a big sip, then gulps another, then puts it on the floor.

Abby follows her out of the locker room. She holds the red railing and walks, looking down at each step. She forgets where she is going.

"Come on," Jenna says, and Abby tries to listen. Jenna takes her sleeve and pulls her, pushing the door open.

The bonfire on the field is lighting up the sky. Each step Abby takes makes the whole world shake. She feels it in her jaw as she walks toward the fire.

There is some kind of banner ahead. Names being called.

"Come on!" she hears Jenna in front of her, pulling her away from the light and back toward the side of the school.

There are already people behind the red doors, standing on the steps, even though the Pep Rally is out by the fields. Abby leans against the wall and takes out a cigarette.

"Light?" someone says and lights her cigarette.

She does not know who. She feels herself slumping against the wall, then sitting. She reaches into her backpack but the bottle is not there.

She looks at the woods, out toward the Living Room. The tree branches have faded into the sky.

"Abby," Jenna says. "Are you OK?" Abby takes a drag of her cigarette and looks down at her legs. She does not think about her face the way she usually does. She is not thinking of the way she seems when she looks up at Jenna and says, "You feelin' it?"

Jenna laughs and slides down the wall to sit next to her.

"You are fucked, girl," she says, taking Abby's cigarette from her to light one of her own.

"Are you?" Abby asks.

"Hell yeah!" Jenna says.

Abby leans over and puts her head on Jenna's shoulder for a second. Then Jenna gets up and grabs Abby's hand to pull her up.

"C'mon," she says. "Let's go to the Living Room!"

Jenna holds Abby's hand as they go into the woods. There are so many roots, and Abby stumbles, holding on to trees with her other hand, holding tight to Jenna.

"Slow down!" she says.

She cannot keep up. She lets go of a tree, of Jenna's hand, and falls. She rips her jeans.

Abby looks up and begins to laugh. There is some kind of light ahead, coming from the Living Room, from behind Jenna's head. She cannot see her face, she can just hear Jenna laughing, see her silhouette, feel her hand.

When Jenna kneels down the light is bright and there are voices.

Jenna touches Abby's knee through her jeans, she can feel it.

"Just your luck," Jenna says.

25.

Headie opens her eyes and looks up at the ceiling. She is on the floor, her head almost beneath the kitchen table.

She makes fists with both her hands. Had she been asleep? She cannot remember how she got there.

The lights are still on and it is still dark out. Or dark out again. She is wearing nightclothes, so perhaps she had been getting ready for bed.

Headie turns over, leaning on her hand, steadying herself sideways. She reaches to the chair to pull herself up, but her legs feel heavy. She looks down at them, looking like her legs always have, but they do not move. They are like prosthetic legs, she thinks. Like old, ugly, lady prosthetics.

She tries to wiggle her toes but cannot. She moves her hips (they are working) and realizes she is wet. The carpet around her is wet too. She has peed herself and the carpet is stapled to the floor. She smells the room— it is her smell.

She is tired. She lies back down and reaches for the computer. She does not feel panicked—she feels strangely calm. She pulls the computer toward her and opens it. The screen is all black.

She quickly presses the button. The *ooohhmmm* sound comes on and she is relieved.

From: headragoldstein@aol.com
To: millieschwartz@aol.com

MILLIE IA M ON THE FLLOOR

Headie pushes the computer away, closes her eyes, and lies back down. She hates feeling wet.

She tries again to move her feet. She feels them a tiny bit, as if they have just fallen asleep and need waking up. Perhaps all her crawling was just preparing her for this.

She lets her eyes roll back into her head. She has time. Her death will not be a surprise.

Not like Gene's, she thinks, whose death had been sudden. Things had had to change quickly. She had to take care of Jeffrey—he was only a teenager. She had to find another man.

That time in her life felt full of worry. She had hoped to avoid it—she had felt it after she moved into her sister's house and did what she had to so as not to feel it again.

Lilac died only a week after Headie moved to Naomi's. The night the hospital called with the news, Headie found Gene in the backyard of her sister's house, eating dirt. It was late, everyone was asleep, and she had been woken by the screen door slamming.

Once outside she saw him, almost animal-like, his eyes watering, wearing striped pajamas. Headie kept her hands crossed on her stomach. He looked up but kept going, digging a hole and putting the dirt into his mouth.

Headie sat on the grass beside him in her nightgown. She could feel the wet ground underneath her.
Once she sat, he looked at her. He stopped eating dirt
and instead just whimpered. He looked like he wanted
her to say something; he would not unlock his eyes
from hers, even after she looked down, embarrassed,
and then looked away.

Headie had never seen a man cry. She had to do
something, so she took Gene's hands. He let her hold
them a moment, then he lay down on his back and
pulled the grass up with his fists.

The wind blew and Headie listened to Gene. His
sobbing was strange. It came out in long, even moans,
then two short gasps and a noisy breath.

"Sssshhhhh," Headie said. She did not want him to
wake the neighbors.

"I c-c-can't," he said, looking up at her. Snot
dripped down his nose.

Gene kneeled in front of Headie with his arms out.
"C-c-can you h-h-hug me?" he asked.

Headie could hug him, but not hard the way he
hugged her, taking his large hands and wrapping them
around her ribs. She thought if he squeezed any harder
she would have to tell him that she was pregnant.

Headie's shoulder was wet with snot and tears.
Gene's breath was hot on her neck.

"Wh-wh-what now?" he asked, rubbing her back,
then backing up and looking right at her. Headie looked
down to where his thick stubby penis surprised her,
sticking out from the pajama slit.

She got down on her knees next to him and gently helped him lean back. She straddled him and leaned over him and put him inside her and moved.

"Oh," he said, three times, and then it was over. He lay back down, still crying.

That night, Headie left her future husband in the backyard while she went back in to clean up. Soon he would see she was pregnant, and he would have to come inside.

Headie breathes deep, thinking of death, but then the dancers come. This time they are singing. It is a lovely tune, something that sounds like a Hebrew song she knew. She hears the word *Zion*; the song is slow, but they are not moving to the beat. They are singing slowly, lined up boy-girl, boy-girl. The girls in their colored dresses, the boys in their tuxedos. They are kicking their legs quickly, still singing the slow song. It is such a lovely song—Headie wishes she knew the words.

Headie watches, as if she is a spectator standing on the edge of the stage. That is the way she feels, as if the dancers are above her, as if she is looking up at them, an audience member.

"Zion . . ." they sing in harmony.

Headie looks for a space between them, a hand that will lift her up, but no one seems to see her. Everyone is keeping time.

26.

Whispers . . . crossing over each other . . .

So many tones of "hussssssshshhhhh . . ."

A crackle of leaves. She is not cold. No.

The sounds again . . .

. . . . shhhhhhhhhhhh

27.

Livia gets in the car, turns on the headlights (it is dark now), and drives out of Simone's driveway. She feels like she might cry.

Her color and design books are back in their same place, next to her on the front seat. She turns onto the road and checks her phone.

There are two messages from Jeffrey:

"Hi, Liv, where are you? I'm on my way to mother's. She fell . . . I'm not sure what's going on yet. I'm in the car on the way. Where are you?? Ugh . . . I'll call later and let you know. Call me as soon as you get this."

and

"Liv, Where ARE you? Call me back!!!"

Livia quickly calls Jeffrey.

"Hi. What happened?" she asks.

She can hear him turn the talk radio down in the car.

"Millie got an email from my mother. It said something about her being on the floor, so she got the neighbor to go over and they found her on the floor in the kitchen, passed out."

"Oh my God!" Livia says. She has a strange feeling, a bit like excitement. Her heart races.

"I should be up there in about an hour and a half. I'm about to shoot The Gap now."

The Gap. On the drive to the Poconos from New York, you have to go down into a valley. At the bottom there is a rest stop with a small creek called The Gap. Once you're done going to the bathroom, getting a soda, maybe putting your feet in the stream, you have to get back in the car again, go back into the mountains.

For some reason Jeffrey always makes a big deal about The Gap. He got Abby into it when she was small. She'd ask when they would get there.

"We're about to shoot it, hon," he would say.

Livia never knew what he was talking about. Why was it being shot? They were driving to a rest stop with a snack machine. For Livia it was a marker: halfway there or halfway home.

"She's in the hospital," Jeffrey says, "but she's stable. The doctor says she's in and out of consciousness."

"OK," Livia says.

"So I'll call you when I get there and let you know," Jeffrey says.

"OK. Call me," Livia says. They say goodbye and hang up.

Livia turns onto the Causeway. She thinks about Headie, alone in the hospital. She thinks of her passed out. She can't remember ever walking in on Headie sleeping; it is hard to imagine. It is hard to imagine Headie letting things go on around her, not bossing someone around.

She can't imagine Headie dying or even getting sick. She is always so busy.

When Livia's parents were dying they had nurses around the clock. Apparently, at one point, her mother had promised her father she would never put him in a nursing home, so they stayed in their large apartment with live-in caretakers.

It was weird when the nurses were there. The women were always nice, always from the Caribbean, and always wore white outfits as if they were in an actual nursing home. Livia wondered what they did when she wasn't there; if they were as attentive to her parents (going deaf and senile at the same time, as if one could not live without the other) as they seemed, or if they sat around ignoring them, playing cards, as soon as she left.

Livia had what Dr. Courtenay had called "mixed feelings" about her parents. But Livia did not feel like the feelings were so mixed. The "feelings" felt angry and finite. When she thought about her parents, when Dr. Courtenay asked, she would talk mostly of her mother.

Livia drives toward town. She pulls into the bright parking lot of the 7-Eleven and goes inside to the chips aisle. She waits until the people at the front counter are gone before she brings her two bags of chips and pre-made onion dip to the counter.

Back in the car Livia opens a bag.

When they were first together, after the sex had died down, Livia thought that she and Jeffrey had the same relationship with food. She ate as much as he did:

half a pizza watching TV, tons of nachos with matching margaritas out to dinner.

But a year into their relationship, over General Tso's chicken, peanut noodles, and a pupu platter, she realized he had stopped eating while she was placing the second dumpling of the platter (the second one of two) into her mouth.

Livia puts the other bag of chips on top of the design books. She wonders where Jeffrey is, then thinks of Gail, lying on her old couch, picturing all the wrong colors. She thinks of tying Gail up, making her listen, bringing a slide projector to their house and showing color slides on the wall while holding Gail's eyes open. Saying "See?" Making Gail nod.

Livia drives through town. A Friday night. There are bars with people standing outside of them. There is a sign at the intersection: Happy Homecoming!

After the attempt, Livia would think about being away from Jeffrey often. Sometimes she wished he would die, and sometimes she thought maybe she should just go somewhere, leave him and Abby alone. She figured she would secure a good nanny first, and then move to Northern California. She knew that Jeffrey would give her money if she needed it.

But she had only thought that way for a short time. Abby would hate her, she knew, if she left. Livia knew that mothers who leave are never loved, not like fathers, who are always searched for and mostly forgiven. Only a terrible mother would leave her child. When she told Dr. Courtenay about wishing to go, she could tell he thought she was bad.

In some ways this was fine. At that time she didn't mind him thinking that. Jeffrey thought so, and Abby, she was sure, thought so too. It felt like the perfect time, then, to go.

But she didn't.

Livia pulls into her driveway and reaches for one last chip (she is three quarters finished), then puts all the chip bags into the plastic bag. The house has hardly any lights on. She turns to park in front of the garage and her headlights shine on Jorgen, standing in front of it.

Livia gasps and quickly rolls up the chips and sticks them in her purse.

"You scared me, Jorgen!" she says, opening the door, getting out of the car.

"Hello Livia, can I help you?" he says, putting out his arms.

Livia tells him he can take the design books in.

"Were you waiting for something?" she calls behind her as he follows her in the back door.

"Yes, Livia," Jorgen says, putting the books on the kitchen table. "I am supposed to have one of the cars tonight for my night off."

"Oh," Livia says, walking to the bedroom and opening the door, throwing the chips bag onto the bed, then coming back out where Jorgen is still standing in the kitchen.

"Jeffrey's mother is sick. He had to go to Pennsylvania to see her in the hospital."

"Oh, I am sorry," he says, looking down at his feet. She sees he is wearing those silly rubber sandals. Where was he planning to go wearing them?

"Ummm, just take my car," Livia says, giving him the keys.

"Thank you!" Jorgen says, taking the keys and running out the door. She hears the car start.

Livia goes back into the bedroom. The house is quiet. Abby is out somewhere. She is alone.

Livia opens the chips and gets into bed (Jorgen can clean the sheets before Jeffrey gets back). She eats with the TV on, then goes out to the liquor cabinet and opens a bottle of good red wine—wine that someone gave them, probably a client of Jeffrey's.

Livia does not know the difference between subtleties of tastes but, pouring the wine into a mug and bringing it back in the bedroom, she does know the difference between cheap wine (the kind that gives you headaches) and what she is drinking now. She sips, trying to imagine what Simone would tell her it tastes like (smoke? licorice?), and then drinks the whole cup and pours herself another.

Livia is alone. She leans back and puts her feet beneath the covers, turns off the TV, then leans over and gets her laptop.

From livia@liviathedecorator.com
To: headragoldstein@aol.com
Dear Headie—

I am so sorry you fell. I know Jeffrey is there right now, and that he is helping you.

I had a terrible day today, and I am sorry that I am not there too. But Jeffrey left before he got in touch with me.

I was at my new clients' house. They are lesbians—the ones with the beautiful old house. I'm not sure I told you about how they are lesbians, but anyway, they are very nice (at least the one I was initially working with, named Simone, is). Her lover,

Livia stops and pours herself another glass. She can hear the white noise from her computer, but otherwise the house is quiet. She doesn't like it. She turns the TV back on.

Gail, is another story. She is very domineering, really "the man" of the relationship. She is very beautiful—you would never know she was a lesbian—but she questioned me in a way, today, that was very insulting. I am hoping that Simone will get her to trust me. I have been having so much success with my decorating business, and it would be a real shame if one woman was to ruin it for me.

Livia stops again. She thinks about going into the living room to eat. It has been so long since she has binged anywhere in her house other than her bedroom or late-late at night in the kitchen. She thinks about going into the den and sitting the way a normal person would sit who sometimes had chips for a snack.

Anyway, I'm sure Jeffrey is almost there. He will make sure that you are fine and comfortable in the hospital. He loves you very much.
Much love,
Liv

Livia closes up the chips and drinks another glass of wine. Suddenly she wants a cigarette. Abby has one, she thinks. Why had she not thought of this before? She walks up the stairs with her mug, opening the closed door of her daughter's bedroom.

When was the last time she was here, in Abby's bedroom, alone? Has she ever actually been alone in it? There are wet towels and clean clothes on the floor. Livia steps over them and crosses the room, going straight for her desk drawer. The desk drawer seems like the place: it is the place Livia kept her stashes when she had them.

She opens the drawer but there are only pens and pencils, bubble gum wrappers, lipstick and blush (she didn't know Abby wore makeup). It makes her feel strange, knowing that her daughter has other hiding places.

Livia goes to the underwear drawer. Inside, she finds a black lacey thong and a purple bra that looks like it would not even cover her daughter's nipples.

Livia has not done the laundry in years. She wonders what Jorgen thought, cleaning this lingerie. Perhaps Abby Woolited them? Perhaps she didn't care.

Livia drinks the rest of her wine, looks at herself in Abby's mirror, and imagines she is her daughter. She wonders if the mirror makes her look thinner or fatter. She is still in the outfit from the day (a carefully chosen black skirt and red shirt). The outfit, she realizes now, was a waste. To impress them she should have worn a tennis skirt, or perhaps jogging pants; something that made her look strong, in touch with her body.

Livia takes off her shirt and throws it on the floor with Abby's clothes. If she were Abby, she would come into her room, take off her sweater, and put her cigarettes where? She takes off her skirt and stockings. Where?

There are no cigarettes in any of her clothes drawers (of course—her daughter is too smart for that. All her clothes would smell.)

She goes for the closet.

She looks behind the hanging clothes, clothes she hasn't seen Abby wear in years, clothes they bought together, when Abby was more feminine and wore dresses.

Behind the clothes are shoeboxes. She opens one and then another but they are all filled with shoes she doesn't wear. Then she finds them: a carton with matches in her Bat Mitzvah shoebox (where are the Bat Mitzvah shoes?). A carton of Marlboro Lights! Livia's old brand.

On her way across the room to the window, she sees herself in the mirror. She is in her bra and underwear.

She is still pretty, but not as pretty as she used to be. She walks closer to the mirror and turns around to see her ass. She has lost something, but she isn't sure what. She wishes she had a word for what it is that is gone. It is more than "youth," or different than that. She wonders if it is something that has been added, or something taken away. She is rounder, which is something more, but her eyes have hollowed, so she is something less.

She pinches her sides, turns from the mirror, and goes to Abby's window, opening up the screen. She kneels, lights a cigarette from her daughter's pack, and leans out.

The air is a bit cold. It is completely dark outside. She can hear cheering from the school.

She is glad Abby isn't into sports. She would have to go to games. When Abby was little she played soccer, and Livia had to go each weekend. It was boring, sitting on the sidelines on a picnic blanket, waiting for time-outs and for innings to end to sit with her daughter and watch her eat cut-up oranges, then go back out to the field.

Sometimes, when Livia watched her daughter, it looked like even she was bored. She was a timid player, always on the defense, but never the goalie. She watched Abby look up at the sky and at her feet when the action was not near her. Sometimes she would do cartwheels or spin on the back of her cleats.

Sometimes Jeffrey came to the games, but usually it was Livia's job. Jeffrey said he needed some time alone which she gave him on Saturday mornings while she watched their daughter spin in circles on the soccer field.

She was glad Abby quit soccer. She'd preferred when Abby was in plays, but she stopped that too.

Livia leans her head out the window and smokes into the air. No one can see her, she knows, she is alone, but if they could, she wonders if they would want her. She wonders if Simone or Gail would find her sexy, her hair down, in just a bra and panties, leaning out the window.

There is a little ledge outside Abby's window, and next to it, Livia sees, a little glass filled with cigarette butts. It is one of their juice glasses, glasses they apparently don't use enough as she has never noticed one was missing. Not that that is something she would notice, really.

Livia lifts her leg out the window, straddling the window for a second, then lifts her other leg out to sit on the ledge, her feet dangling. She ashes in the glass her daughter ashes in on top of all the cigarettes her daughter has already smoked.

Livia thinks of Gail and Simone again and wonders what they are doing right now. Perhaps they are finishing dinner (some kind of fish or chicken dish, light, with salad, and perhaps cantaloupe for dessert). They are probably sitting in their empty den drinking an after-dinner glass of wine. Perhaps they are on the couch, next to each other, their bare feet touching. Perhaps Gail has her legs and feet on Simone's lap, or Simone is playing with Gail's blonde curls.

Perhaps Simone is looking at the fine blonde hairs on Gail's legs, thinking about how she would like to touch them, while Gail says, "I think we should find another interior decorator."

Perhaps Simone stops twisting Gail's hair, stops looking at her leg, and thinks of Livia.

"Oh, no, Livia is going to be great, hon. She has some great ideas."

Perhaps Gail sits up, takes her legs from Simone's lap, and says, "Simone, remember—you are too trusting. We don't know this woman, and we haven't even seen her portfolio. At least let's gets some other proposals before we make a decision."

Perhaps Simone is looking at Gail, thinking how her beauty never gets boring, how she loves to look at her, and kiss her, and make love.

Perhaps Simone says, at this moment, while Livia is on the windowsill of her own house in her underwear, "OK, let's see who else is out there."

Livia quickly puts her cigarette out in the cup. She turns and puts her leg in through the window, then climbs back into the house. She closes the screen and the window behind her, then gets the mug and her clothes from the floor, and runs downstairs to her phone.

She hits SIMONES to dial and the phone begins to ring, but immediately there is another call, an UNKNOWN. Livia waits another ring, but since it might be Jeffrey at the hospital, she picks it up.

"Is this Mrs. Schecter?" someone says as soon as she switches lines.

"Yes," Livia says.

"This is Mrs. Eldridge, the school principal. Your daughter is in the hospital. She may have alcohol poisoning."

"What?" Livia says, trying to picture Mrs. Eldridge.

"Mrs. Schecter, I am calling from the school to tell you that your daughter is at the hospital. She was taken from the school in an ambulance and was unconscious."

"The school?" Livia says.

"Yes, Mrs. Schecter, it is Pep Rally tonight. Your daughter was at school."

Livia hangs up and calls Jorgen, who tells her he is right around the corner. He will be home in a minute.

She calls Jeffrey, who does not answer. Then, calls him again. She runs downstairs, puts on sweats, sits on the couch, gets up, and looks in the fridge. She dials Jeffrey again and listens to his voicemail, then leaves him a message, trying to explain.

"The principal called. From Abby's school and now she is at the hospital. I am going there as soon as Jorgen gets home. Call me as soon as you get this."

She feels the wine. She wants to run upstairs to get more cigarettes.

The phone rings again. The number is UN-KNOWN.

"Hello?" Livia says, pacing in the kitchen.

"Mrs. Schecter?" a woman asks.

"Yes?"

"This is Mrs. Eldridge again. I am at the hospital. I am unsure if you realize what is going on here, but I urge you, again, to come here as soon as you can." Livia sits down. The principal, talking to her this way, makes her feel like she might cry. She can feel it in her voice. She clears her throat.

"I am waiting for our au pair to bring the car home. I am trying to get there as fast as I can."

"Oh, I see. You should have said something. Do you have anyone else to call?"

"No," Livia says, "My husband . . ."

The car lights shine through the windows and Livia hangs up the phone and runs out to the driveway.

Jorgen gets out.

"She's going to be OK," he says, standing as if he wants to talk. Livia does not look at him; she is angry at him. What took him so fucking long?

She gets into the driver's seat and goes, past the stop sign at the end of the road without stopping, driving as fast as she can.

28.

Abby opens her eyes and sees her pubic hair. She sees white sheets too, but they are not covering it.

She is lying in a bed and the lights are bright. A woman is leaning over her with a round yellow button.

SMILE: IT MAKES YOU FEEL GOOD! it says.

Abby reaches out for the button and touches it.

"You like that?" the woman asks.

Abby tries to focus on the woman but her face seems too close. She looks to her right. Jenna is in another bed, next to her.

"Jenna," Abby moans. Her throat hurts.

She looks down to where her pubic hair is, but now it is covered by a sheet.

"We're in trouble," she hears Jenna say.

Abby looks at the sheet, her pubic hair beneath it. Everything is blurry, and then black . . .

"Abby."

It is her mother, suddenly next to her. It seems like she has just appeared: her mother with smudged mascara.

Abby reaches up and pats her mother's hair.

"Where's Dad?" she asks. It feels hard to talk—her mouth is too big and heavy.

Abby's mother pats her head back. She leans in and kisses both of her cheeks, hard and wet.

Abby turns to look at Jenna again. Jenna is not laughing. The room is very bright.

"Where's Dad?" she asks again.

She looks at her arm. It seems far away. There is an IV in her hand, but it doesn't hurt. She looks at the woman with the button again, who seems to be coming close, then going back. She cannot believe how she has just been lying here—where had she been?—with her pubic hair showing.

She looks back at the nurse, who seems to understand.

"You're in the hospital," the woman says. She does not seem angry. She seems like someone's mom. "You drank too much."

Abby's mother's face, up close, nods to her. Abby burps.

"I'm sorry," she says.

Before they moved to Long Island they lived in an old Victorian house in Philadelphia. They lived in a neighborhood, and the street had many big houses. There was not much land between each house, but there were small yards. They had a wraparound porch with a swing that made the windows behind it rattle if you swung too far back.

For a long time Abby's mother had been obsessed with table manners. In the old house in the big kitchen, her mother would make her practice.

Abby was not good at table manners. At first she couldn't cut her London broil; then she didn't sit with her hands in her lap. She always forgot which way to set the table (the spoon on the right; fork on the left? Or vice-versa?)

She chewed with her mouth open. She could not blow her nose without her parents' help.

When they re-did the kitchen in Philadelphia, her mother had Formica counters put in. The counters were a strange burnt-orange color that Abby didn't like.

Her mother had an extra counter put in away from the appliances, facing the far wall. She had Abby's father hang corkboard strips above it so that they could thumbtack Abby's drawings to it. She put all of Abby's art supplies on the counter and called it the "art station."

At first, Abby liked the art station. She could sit and draw while her mother tried to cook. But when the manners obsession started, the art station quickly changed.

If Abby put her elbows on the table or talked while she was chewing, she was sent—plate, milk and all—over to face the wall. Her art station transformed into what her mother called "the pigpen."

The pigpen was for children who had no manners. When you were sent there, your parents talked as if you didn't exist. Sometimes Abby's mother would make a comment about pigs. No one could see what she was doing, so Abby would play with the food on her plate.

"Abby?" she hears her mother say.

Abby opens her eyes and remembers thinking of Philadelphia.

"See?" the nurse says to her mother. "I told you, she'll be fine now. She's just in and out—her system is trying to recover."

Abby wishes her mother were like the nurse, saying things in a way that made you believe them. Her mother is holding her hand too tight.

Abby looks to the right again and sees Jenna, turned away. She looks down and sees she is wearing a hospital bracelet.

"How do you feel?" her mother asks. Her mother no longer has the mascara all over her face—it has been cried off.

Abby says nothing. She doesn't feel like speaking. She feels too tired.

Then suddenly there is Chess. Next to her mother. They look strange side by side.

". . . a friend, Abby," she hears her mother say.

There is Chess. She sees the number of his football uniform.

"Hi Abby," he says. Abby feels her mother's smooth hand release her own and feels Chess's dry one replace it.

Chess and her mother, close enough to be in a photo together and not look like strangers.

"You can bring her home in a few hours," she hears the nurse say.

"You're OK," Chess says, and she believes him.

29.

Headie can feel herself moving. She can feel her body, wet, in the cold air. She cannot see, and she is not sure if her eyes are open or not.

She senses a blanket, but she cannot hear. It is as if she is only nerves. She wonders if she is dead.

She is not sure if she is moving forward or backward. It is nice—she does not feel sick. Instead it is as if she is already asleep and yet still sleepy, but not in a tired way. It is as if she is in a big bassinet made just for her, and whoever is rocking it is an angel.

Headie can tell she is breathing. She does not see a white light. Instead, the dancers begin to appear. Out of the blackness they are coming toward her.

They are especially colorful and dancing especially fast. Some of the people look familiar, like she knows them but has never seen them dance before.

They are dancing so quickly, the girls twirling and twirling, it is hard to recognize anyone. The men's feet are moving in ways that do not look possible. They are twisting their limbs up and around, kicking their feet out backward.

She feels wherever she is moving from, moving to, suddenly stop, and at the same time all the dancers fall forward, as if they were on a bus that just braked. They all lie on the black floor. Finally still, she begins to focus. There is Lilac wearing a lilac sweater, and next to her is Gene.

Farther back is Allen. She did not know he could dance that way.

"Allen!" she tries to yell to him, then worries that she is hurting Gene's feelings. She has had dreams like that, where Gene found out about Allen. They were dreadful dreams.

Headie feels herself moving again. The dancers feel it too. They stand, and Headie reaches out for Allen. She yells his name again and again, but he is dancing with someone else.

They begin dancing too fast; they all swirl together. Again, they become a colorful blur.

Headie tries to shake her head the way she usually does. She wishes they would stop.

Then suddenly, again, they do. They fall to the ground like before, but this time they slide forward, as if off some kind of black ledge. It reminds her of that theater Jeffrey and Livia took her to once. It was called Black Box theater. The stage was black and Headie fell asleep.

She sees Allen and tries to reach for him. The feeling is familiar: reaching that way, wanting that way. Headie remembers the feeling she had when she had wanted a man. It was as if the top of her chest was swelling. It was like something was trying to get out of her. She was too big inside, she thought, when she felt that way. It had been such a long time, she suddenly feels faint even though she is sure she is lying down.

She has not felt this way in years, this yearning. Not since Allen waved to her in the bank when she had come to town for her father's funeral. Her father had died quickly, only two years after Gene. She had been there a week with her stepmother, Janet (a boring woman, nice enough, not nosy, but no match for her father), and Naomi, who all took turns being by his side. It was hard for Headie to put the feelings that she had for this man who she loved when she was a girl toward this crumpled, dying man who had left her for Janet. Still, the three women had all cried together in the waiting room, their arms around each other, with an empty space the size of the man who had left them in the middle.

Headie was forty-five and all Allen did was wave. She had not put makeup on since the morning, and she waited in the bank line with her eyes on her shoes. She had not seen him since she left—not for almost twenty years.

But when she got back into her car, he was getting into his. He waved again and she waved back and shut her car door. She concentrated on buckling herself in.

Her chest felt like it was leaving her, as if her thoughts were inside it too. She sat in the car for a minute, trying to catch her breath. She imagined following his shiny green Cadillac all the way to his big house with all its empty rooms and his shiksa wife, older now, waiting for him with a Danish and coffee.

Headie's chest or her heart or whatever it was inside her that she felt when she closed her eyes went with him into his house where he sat on his couch, loosened his tie, turned on the TV, while his wife mixed herself a drink and went into the bedroom. Headie imagined being next to him, on the floral couch, safe beneath his outstretched arm.

Everything is black but Headie is still unsure if her eyes are closed. Something has covered her again, and she is warm. Someone touches her hand—it is a man's hand—dry, a bit hairy, strong.

The hand touches her fingers. She would give up her sight if whoever was holding her hand would just keep it there forever. She would die—she would be happy to, even—if she could just dance with Allen.

She holds on to the hand, but it feels as if she cannot truly grasp it. Like when Allen took her hand, back then, the second time. His hand was strong and gripped hers harder. It was that same feeling of being unable to hold it back hard enough, afraid it would stop holding hers if she did.

Headie had been overtired from her father's funeral, and a little drunk on white wine. Allen had knocked on the window of her car in the parking lot of the bank while she was imagining him at home. She rolled the window down and he gave his condolences. He was older, with less hair, and fatter, but still him. He asked if she would like to visit his wife, who was sick, so she followed him to his house.

"Shhhh," Allen had said outside the front door of his house. He took her hand, walking through his living room with its tan carpet and matching tan sofas (not floral like she had imagined) and a cabinet filled with colorful glass that Headie caught out of the corner of her eye.

He pointed to the stairs and whispered, "She's asleep."

For years Headie had thought about him each time she touched herself. For years and years he was the only fantasy she had: both of them in the back room of the store, knocking against the winter clothes.

He pulled her past their yellow kitchen with its matching yellow flowered curtains and yellow table-cloth, into a blue-painted room with a pale blue bed-spread.

"We can talk in here," he said, and she looked at him, wondering where his wife was.

Headie looked around. She did not know where to sit. He motioned to the bed so she sat on it. He sat beside her and took her hand.

She did not want to look up. She was embarrassed with no makeup.

Allen picked up her chin and kissed her, his tongue gentle and smooth. Then he stood up in front of her and undid his belt. He took himself out of his brown pants and the checkered boxers she could see a tiny bit of before she closed her eyes and tasted him. It had been so long since she had tasted a man.

She sucked on him. She wanted to make him love her. He held her head and made noises that she hoped his wife could not hear. Then he stopped her and knelt down slowly, taking off her pantyhose. He looked up at her and smiled.

"What do you like now?" he asked. "Is this what you like?" and he slowly pulled down her panties and gently moved his tongue against her.

Gene had never done this to her. Naomi had told her about David doing it, but Headie couldn't imagine why a man would want to.

"You taste good," he said, and Headie tried to believe him, lying back and closing her eyes. Her father was dead. Allen remembered.

Allen pulled himself up and put himself inside her. She opened her eyes to watch him, to see that it was real. She moved against him and watched his open mouth and his cavities, his lips that did not kiss her.

"Oh Headie!" he said. "Do you like this now?" he opened his eyes, looking at her.

"Yes," she said. She liked it. She loved it. She wanted his wife to stick to her bed forever. She wanted to tie his wife down. She wanted this man, this father of her only son, who let himself weaken in her arms, collapsing on top of her, then moving next to her, breathing, to keep touching her hand and tickling her fingers.

"Wow," he said, out of breath. She had gotten him in his second season.

Headie watched his chest slowly begin to reach its normal breathing rhythm. She watched as he turned to her and hugged her. He touched the back of her head.

"I'm sorry," he said again, "about your father."

Headie reached around to touch his back.

She remembered her father. She felt like crying.

"I'm sorry too," she said.

•

Headie feels the hand. She is warm now, covered in something, she thinks, but she does not feel scared. The hand is still there, but it is not squeezing tight enough.

She wonders if when she dies she will see Gene and have to tell him. Perhaps he will take her hand and they will dance and she will whisper it into his ear and he will forgive her.

She hopes he understands. She had been his wife for so long, she had loved him as much as she could. She could tell him she loved him—it was true. When he died she did not know what to do.

When she saw him on the floor, she got down next to him and said his name. She turned him over and looked at his pale face. She slapped it and he did nothing.

"Gene?" she said again.

He did not answer.

Headie had been out getting groceries and was late. Jeffrey was at baseball practice and did not see Gene dead. He was lucky, Headie thought, because Gene as he lay on the floor—face down, his scotch spilled next to him, his head in the kitchen, his body in the living room—was not something a son should see.

The music was on when Headie came home and she wondered if Gene had been dancing. Perhaps he was imagining Lilac, she thought later, imagining holding her hand and doing old steps. Perhaps he got too excited.

She got up and called the police. She turned off the music. She looked at the clock on the wall and cleaned up the scotch. She sat on the couch and looked at Gene, her sweet and loyal husband. She remembered how David had told her that when Gene was little he pulled out all his eyelashes in his sleep.

And when he used to stutter. Before he went inside her for the first time, his thoughts did not reach into the world, or to another person, without having to travel through his rocky mouth. She looked at his dead body, and thought that that was probably why he had danced when he was younger. When he danced he was able to move to the beat and keep the beat inside at the same time. It was not often that someone's outsides matched their insides like that. She wondered if now his insides matched his outsides just the same.

While Headie waited for the ambulance she looked down at her husband, his face gray, his stubble growing in, his mouth open like he was snoring. She cried because he had not lived the way he wanted to, and she cried because she had made him think that she loved him. She cried, and the ambulance came and took him away, and she cried because he never had a son.

30.

Livia stands at the entranceway to the hospital room and sees Abby in a white bed with an IV, looking like she is sleeping or dead. She is on her back, tubes up her nose.

Livia walks slowly toward her daughter. She feels as if she might pass out. The nurse who brought her in explained that Abby had her stomach pumped.

She sits down in the chair next to the bed and watches her daughter's eyelids flutter. She wonders if she is dreaming. She takes Abby's hand and wishes she had not drunk so much wine. She cannot get her head in place. Her daughter . . . Jeffrey . . .

"The doctor will be here in a minute," the nurse says.

Livia looks at her. She has colorful buttons all over her white uniform.

"Is she OK?" Livia begins to cry.

"She'll be fine," the nurse says, adjusting Abby's pillow, checking her IV.

The doctor walks in. He is in a suit with a stethoscope and a white coat. He has gray hair and looks like a good husband and father.

"She's going to be fine, Mrs. Schecter," he says as soon as she looks up. "She drank a very large amount of alcohol. We had to pump her stomach, and she will be sore. But she will be fine."

"Why is she sleeping?" Livia asks. She looks at her daughter. She cannot remember the last time she saw her asleep. Her skin is beautiful, flushed.

"She's just recovering. But everything is fine." He says something to the nurse and leaves, and Livia looks back at Abby.

Livia looks around the room. On the other side there is another bed with another girl in it, facing the wall, her brown hair loose on the pillow.

Livia feels a hand on her back and lets it pat her a few times before she looks up to see a young-looking woman with wrinkles around her eyes. She has brown hair cut in a bob.

"I'm Jenna's mother," the woman says.

Livia stands and turns and looks closer at the other bed. The girl is facing her now. It is Jenna. A man (her father?) is standing next to her bedside. Jenna also has an IV, but she is awake and looking at Livia and her mother. She is listening.

Livia turns from Jenna's mother but does not say anything. Her daughter is not listening.

She pats Abby's hand.

"Abby, wake up," she says. She has the urge to slap her cheeks, but instead takes the washcloth that the nurse gave her and touches it to her forehead.

She watches as Abby's eyes flutter. The nurse comes over and takes her other hand. She says Abby's name loudly, and Abby opens her eyes and burps. Livia watches her daughter try to focus, her tongue searching in her mouth.

"Where's Dad?" Abby whispers. Livia leans in and kisses her on both cheeks. She does not answer.

"I'm sorry," Abby says, then closes her eyes again.

"See?" the nurse says, "I told you she'll be fine now. She's just in and out."

A boy is suddenly next to her. He is pink-cheeked, in a sports uniform. He is the one Livia saw Abby with downtown.

"Chess?" she hears Jenna call from the other end of the room. "Chess?"

The boy looks at Livia.

"I'm Chess," he says, not turning around. "Is she OK?"

Livia looks at the boy. The boy with the Jeep. She nods.

"Honey," Livia says, squeezing her daughter's hand. Her eyes have closed again. "You have a friend, Abby."

"Chess?" she hears Jenna call again from the other end of the room.

Chess turns. "I'll be there in a second," he says, but nicely. He turns back to Abby.

Livia releases Abby's hand and gives it to Chess. She watches as her daughter's eyes open.

"You're OK," he says to her.

Livia's phone rings. It is her husband. She picks it up and tells him that their daughter is in the hospital, has had her stomach pumped, will wake up soon.

"What happened?" he asks.

His voice is shaking.

"I don't know."

"My mother . . ." Jeffrey says.

"I'm going to call you back," Livia says. She hangs up the phone and goes back to her daughter. She takes Abby's hand back from Chess who stands up and walks away.

"Hey girl," she can hear Chess talking to Jenna.

Abby's skin is warmer now. Her eyes flutter. Livia squeezes her hand and releases it, steadily, like a heart-beat.

31.

Abby wakes up to the cheers from the homecoming game. She can hear them from where she is lying down, in her father's study, on the pullout bed. Her mother is lying next to her, staring at nothing.

"Mom?" she says.

She watches her mother's eyes, startled for a second, then focused.

"How are you feeling?" her mother says.

It has been a long time since Abby has been sick, since she has stayed home and lain in bed while her mother (or the au pair) brought her soup.

"I'm OK," Abby says, pulling off the covers. She is wearing some kind of gown that she does not own. She has a hospital bracelet on her arm. Her throat hurts when she talks.

Abby's mother sits up, turning herself so that she is facing Abby. She seems so serious. Abby can't help it: she smirks.

"Abby!" her mother says, slapping her face.

Abby's mouth opens. A tear builds in her eye. Her lip turns up again: she cannot help it.

"Why are you smiling!?" her mother asks, then puts her face in her hands and begins to sob.

"Mom," Abby says, looking at the TV and at her father's desk, wondering where her father is, why he isn't here to comfort her mother. "It's OK."

"You almost killed yourself!"

Her mother's eyes are red and small. She looks the way she did when Abby was younger.

"I'm sorry," Abby says. She swallows. Her voice is hoarse. She touches her throat.

"You had your stomach pumped, Abby." Her mother takes a deep breath and dries her tears. "The doctor said you could have died if no one got you." Abby's mind flashes out to the dark, toward the Living Room, with Jenna. Then someone—Alec?—helping her up, leading her. She was on top, her shirt open, rubbing against him.

"I don't want to have sex," she remembers saying.

"You looked dead," her mother says.

"Where is Dad?" Abby asks. She tries to whisper. Her throat aches.

"Bubbe is sick. She's in the hospital too. It's all a mess. How could you have done this, Abby?"

Abby is unsure what to say. She remembers being out by the red doors at school, then being nowhere.

Her mother is still crying. Her hair is all over the place. Abby has not seen her like this in ages, not in years.

"When is Dad getting home?" Abby asks.

"I said I don't know!" Livia says, reaching over to the desk for tissues.

"No you didn't," Abby says.

Abby stares at her mother. She looks different. Bigger? Smaller? She isn't sure.

When Abby was younger, her mother seemed to become a different size daily. Her smile lines appeared and disappeared, even when she wasn't smiling. She would turn from being black inside and angry to happy, nice, buying Abby presents. It was a quick change that evened out as soon as her father came home.

Abby was scared of her mother for a long time, but at some point she stopped. She couldn't remember when.

Livia begins to cry again.

"You almost died!" she says.

Abby wishes her father were here. She remembers when she was six and her mother got both Abby's and her own ears pierced one day. When her father came home from work and didn't notice her mother's ears, Livia threw a fit, taking the new earrings out of her ears and throwing them on the ground, then taking Abby's out (Abby screaming, crying, *Please don't, Mom!*) and throwing the tiny diamond studs so that they landed beneath the couch.

Her ears were red and sore and her father stood there. Abby ran up to him and hugged him. He petted her head. Her mother lay on the ground, face down, sobbing, and Abby got down near her, but didn't touch her. She looked beneath the dark couch to try and find the shiny earrings.

Abby looks down at her fingers. The maroon nail polish she painted on yesterday before the rally is still there. She begins to pick it off, little flecks dotting the blanket like blood.

Abby watches her mother's eyes stare into space, then back at Abby.

"I'll call him," Abby says.

As she reaches for the phone, Abby's mother grabs her wrist.

"OK. But he's going to be angry," her mother says.

Abby stops and turns again to her mother.

"Why?" she says.

Her mother gives a little laugh. "Because you almost fucking died! Because you were passed out by the back of the school and the teachers had to bring you in and ambulances had to come and you had to have your stomach pumped! What is wrong with you, Abby?"

Abby gets up and runs to her room. She shuts the door, locks it, and goes to her shoebox to get her cigarettes. She opens the window, still in her gown, and goes up to the roof.

She lights a cigarette and takes a drag. Her throat hurts, but it feels good to smoke. She can hear the cheering from the game. She wonders who is winning. She thinks of Chess, running. Does he know?

Abby ashes her cigarette. The stubs in the glass are soggy from dew, except for one. One has lipstick on it. It is red.

Abby picks up the lipsticked cigarette and holds it closer. She has not brought Jenna up to the roof since last week and Jenna's lipstick is pink.

There are the striations of red lips. There is the proof. She pictures her heavy-footed mother climbing out the window. It scares her to think about it.

Because now she knows it's true. Anything can happen. She can die, her Bubbe can die, she can be in the woods and no one can get her, her mother can be happy and sad at the same time, her father can actually be angry at her, her au pair can fool around with her friend, and oh, she forgot: her mother can go into her closet and climb out on her roof. Her mother can smoke her cigarettes.

32.

There is a sound. It is not good or bad. It is even, back and forth, up and down.

It is a soft sound, but Headie concentrates on it. It is rhythmic, but slow.

Headie tries to open her eyes to see it. She wonders if it looks as good as it sounds, but she cannot seem to open her lids. She is tired and stops trying.

Instead, she enjoys the sound. It is like air that is being pulled and pushed. It is refreshing, like waves on a lake, or better: it is what you would hear if you put your ear against a waterbed.

Headie feels a hand again. It is stroking her fingers. She can't remember if it left and then came back or if it has been there this whole time. She wants it there, she just wishes it would be still and squeeze.

When she was married to Gene she preferred to be held, still. With Gene, she learned, when it came to sex she could feel nothing. During sex, she found herself making conscious decisions about what she would do next.

She had always wanted Gene to hold her afterward (or instead). He seemed like the kind of man who would, that night after she had comforted him in the backyard.

That night, after he pulled up his pajamas and followed her into the den, they sat side by side, not saying anything. He was no longer crying; it was enough. She touched his hand, said goodnight, and went to her own room to bed.

The next night she went out into the den again after Naomi and David had gone to sleep. She had been gone during the day, looking for jobs. At dinner she had hardly glanced at him.

But at night, in the den, she took his hand from under his covers where it had been resting, still awake, and led him into her room, where she quickly lifted her big flannel nightgown again and lay down on the bed. He was fumbly and embarrassed, so she took over. Afterward, he lay there, not holding her, so she turned sideways and went to sleep, waiting for him to close the door behind him.

The next morning at breakfast, Gene asked for eggs and then bacon, and Headie, in her robe, turned to look at him. He was looking down at his hands, as if they had done something without him knowing.

He looked up. "I'm not stuttering," he said.

Naomi came into the kitchen.

"I'm not stuttering," he said.

"What happened?" she asked, looking over at Headie. One month later Headie was "sure" she was pregnant; they got married, and Gene never stuttered again.

Headie feels the hand. It is still now, finally. She is warm and feels safe and satisfied. She does not have to clean.

She tries to squeeze it, but she feels her arms not moving. Maybe this is it. Perhaps death is being able to feel and hear but not be able to do anything about it. She wonders if she is wearing her nightgown.

Death is not terrible if it is like this. If this is it, it is not hell. Except if this is it, what about the coffin? She hopes that there is a silky lining.

She tries to squeeze again and hears something: a low deep drone. She has never believed in heaven.

She hears her name, she thinks, and then feels her eyes move, but she does not feel that she can control them. It is as if they are being opened by someone else.

There, a white light. Perhaps there is a heaven.

Or something better, she sees, after the light is gone.

A man. She sees him. He is holding her hand.

A man: blue eyes and dark hair. A familiar smile. Heaven.

"Allen?" she says.

33.

Livia is lying in her bedroom, staring at the print of the man with the globe, when the phone rings.

"Hello?" She picks up quickly, thinking it is Jeffrey.

"Is this Livia Schecter?" a woman's voice says. She hears a slight Long Island accent.

"May I ask who's calling?" Livia says.

"This is Carla Marino, Jenna's mother," the voice says, and Livia flashes back to the night before when Abby was lying, dead, next to Jenna, who was talking in her bed, telling her mother and father she was sorry.

Carla Marino with a face just like her daughter's. A pale blue jacket.

"Hello," Livia says again.

There is a sigh. Livia wonders if a sigh can have an accent.

"I'm calling because the girls cannot see each other anymore. I want to let you know that I don't think your daughter has been a good influence—they are not good influences on each other. Your daughter seems to have quite a problem."

Livia sits up. She thinks again of the woman she is speaking to. She was pale, her lips colorless. Her husband was short, with a beard.

She thinks of Jenna, awake in the bed, while Abby lay silent, her mouth open, sleeping.

"*My* daughter?" Livia says, sitting up and putting her feet on the floor. "My daughter never drank anything before she met Jenna."

The woman sighs again. "I'm not sure that's the case," she says.

Carla Marino looked so young the night before. Why is she talking to Livia like she is a child?

Carla had her husband with her; Livia was alone.

Livia sighs. She can feel the air come back at her from the phone.

"I know for a fact it is. My husband was planning on calling you later today as well," Livia says. "I'm glad we spoke."

"If I find out the two of them are together I'll call you. I hope you'll do the same," Carla Marino says. She gives Livia her number. Livia repeats it but does not write it down.

After she hangs up, Livia lies back on the bed. She can hear Abby moving around above her. She can hear her walk from one part of the floor to the other. She has never thought about it too much before: it's like air conditioning, like white noise, the padding of her daughter's feet in the sky.

She listens now as her daughter moves. She tries to picture where she is. She can see her stopping in front of the mirror to look at herself; she can hear her move from the mirror, maybe, to her desk. Perhaps she is opening the window.

Livia tries to remember the worst thing she ever did that her parents found out about. She tries to think of what her mother did.

She had been caught drunk, with boys, with cigarettes. Livia came out from her father's office with red eyes, after he told her she was a slut, a whore, a disgrace, and her mother ignored her.

Livia did worse things for a while. Before she met Jeffrey, especially. Drugs, sex, more sex. It was Jeffrey who made her see that every man's wife is someone else's slut. She learned this the hard way (there were many men she would never see again).

Jeffrey saw her, clean and beautiful. He saw her "really." He slept with her and watched her and loved her. He brought her back to her own parents and made them see her new too: a bride.

She introduced this new self to his family as well. Her mother-in-law had loved her from the beginning, and when she had Abby, everyone loved her more. They came close to Livia to hold the baby. They watched her nurse, watched her be a mother.

It seemed like other people's fault, sometimes, that she became bad. It was their fault because if they had stayed, she would have stayed the way they saw her. She would have stayed a good mother as long as they hadn't left her alone.

But when they left, she felt it. Black inside. Or the darkest purple mixed with black. She was black inside with organs that floated and had nothing to do with the real problem. Everything worked: her tear ducts, her urinary tract, her breasts full of milk, but she was secretly defective. If they opened her up . . .

When Jeffrey finally saw her in the hospital, all black inside, he stopped loving her. He saw her, *really*. She was sure of it.

Livia can hear Abby opening her window, going out on her roof. She had not recognized this sound before, even though she must have heard it a million times.

Livia wishes there was something that she could do, like go out on the roof and smoke with her daughter. Livia's own mother smoked. She smoked in front of her. She is sure that Carla Marino does not smoke with her daughter. But that does not make her a good mother: she is sure of that too. Livia wishes she had paid more attention to Jenna now. What had she been doing not to notice the girl, the sounds, her daughter?

She had been focused on designing. That was what she was doing. She had been involved with the colors of Simone's home. She had been worrying about paints.

She thinks of a TV show she once saw where some women had to describe themselves. Each one began with "I am a mother . . ."

Livia wonders how she would describe herself.

"I am smart," she thinks. "I am married."

She thinks of other things too (I am interested in dreams—I like art—I am working on my thesis). None of them make her sound like what she wants to sound like. None of them seem enough to describe the person she wants to be.

Livia looks at the print of the man with the globe. Today he looks as if he is giving her the world, not taking it away. The world looks heavy, filled with mothers and daughters. It looks as if it will burst.

So many mothers and daughters. How is it that
there are so many mothers out there, living, and so few
of them dealing with a daughter who almost killed herself with alcohol the night before? How is it that there
are so many daughters out there who have mothers that
do not make them want to do something like that?

Livia picks up the phone and calls Jeffrey. She leaves
a message, telling him to call her, when the other line
beeps.

Livia picks it up. "Hello?"

"Hello, this is Mrs. Eldridge calling again," the
voice says.

Livia sits up and leans over, resting her head on her
palm. She does not say anything.

"I'm calling to tell you that Abigail has been suspended for two days. A tutor will come to your home on
Monday and Tuesday to work with her while she is
out."

"Are there any other punishments I should know
about?" Livia asks. She can hear the annoyance in her
voice, even though she had intended for it to be hidden.
Once it is out there, there is nothing she can do. Out
there, where her voice has landed in Mrs. Eldridge's ear,
she is sure she has become a bad mother.

"No, Mrs. Schecter. Although I have to say that I
highly recommend you have Abigail begin counseling.
This is a serious thing that has happened here."

"I am aware of the seriousness, Mrs. Eldridge. Both
my husband and I are aware of it. We are taking care of
it. I appreciate your concern."

"Please let me know if there is anything the school can do," Mrs. Eldridge says.

"I will. Goodbye." Livia hangs up the phone.

Livia calls Jeffrey again. He picks up.

"Hi. She's awake. The principal called and now she's suspended for two days."

"What?" Jeffrey says. "What do you mean?"

"I mean that she has been suspended. And Carla Marino, Jenna's mother, called to tell us that Jenna is no longer allowed to see Abby and that Abby is a bad influence."

"She's fucking suspended?! Is she kidding? There is no way that Abby is the problem with those two. Anyway, that's fine. I don't want her with that girl either. There wasn't a problem with Abby before Jenna. Don't you think?" Jeffrey asks.

Livia waits. This is the first time Jeffrey has asked her anything about parenting that she can remember.

"Yes," she says, "and I told her that too."

"Good," Jeffrey says. "I'm glad."

Livia turns on her back. Suddenly she feels happy. Then she remembers.

"How is Headie?" she asks.

"She's out of ICU. She sleeps and wakes up. The doctors are still keeping a close eye."

"Then when will you be home?" Livia asks.

"Livia," Jeffrey says, and his old voice, his voice from before this phone call, his voice for years and years, comes back into the phone. "I don't know."

It is an annoyed voice, his voice. It is an exasperated voice. It is a voice of a man who thinks he has to hold the world.

Suddenly she feels like she might cry. The problem is clear. He has not seen his daughter, dead.

"OK," Livia says. "We're fine."

34.

Abby lies on her bed and listens to the cheers from the school. She tries to make herself spin. She closes her eyes to go backwards on the wheel, even though it is not even noon.

Abby tries to spin, but each time she is about to her mind flits to Alec, then to Chess, then to Jenna.

The phone rings.

"Hello?" she says.

"Holy shit!" says Jenna on the line.

"I know," Abby says. "How did that happen?"

"You have NO tolerance, that's how. You almost died, you know," Jenna says.

Abby is quiet. She cannot remember almost dying.

"Thank God for Jorgen," Jenna says.

"Why?"

"You don't remember anything, huh?"

"Not really," Abby says.

"I do," Jenna says. "The whole school saw you all passed out outside the gym. Actually, Alec told me that. And then Chess told me too when he visited me in the hospital."

"Oh," Abby says. Then she remembers: Chess in the hospital. His face, red. Did he say something to her? She cannot remember.

"We're probably not going to be able to hang out anymore."

"Why?" Abby says.

"Are you still drunk?" Jenna asks.

"No," Abby says. "They pumped it out."

"Yes, I *know*," Jenna says. "I was *there*. I didn't have mine pumped though."

"You didn't?" Abby asks. "Why not?"

"Because you drank *way* more," Jenna says, "and you have no tolerance."

Abby suddenly feels sick again. "I have to go," she says.

"OK, but don't call me. My mom won't let me talk to you. I'll call you."

"OK," Abby says.

Abby hangs up the phone and lies back down.

She looks up at the ceiling. It is some kind of stucco. Ugly. She hates this house.

She reaches up with her foot and opens her blind by sticking her toe in the string and pulling. The cheers seem to be getting louder, and she thinks of Chess, playing on the field. She looks out at the trees and wonders if he's winning.

How did she drink so much more? She remembers the bathroom, going down the stairs, outside, the bonfire, bright and exciting in the dark. A little like when she was in *Cinderella*; there was something so strange about being at school at night. It was like you could get caught for something, even if you weren't doing anything wrong.

But she *was* doing something wrong. She drank vodka, then left the locker room. She was outside by the doors, going into the woods with Jenna, then Alec.

She wonders what Alec said to her, how he began talking to her after not talking to her, how she answered him. She does not remember the rest of the walk, or Jenna leaving.

She lets the blind go down with her toe. She closes her eyes and tries to think of something. She sees the bottle, the side of the school, then she remembers looking up, seeing a flashlight. Voices were coming toward her; Alec was on the couch. Then nothing again.

She does not remember the black. She wonders where she went. All these things going on without her. It was like being dead, like being a puppet or a doll. Like being there but not being able to see who is watching you. Like being dead with your watch still ticking.

Anything could have happened, she thinks. Even Chess. Maybe it was him who came down to the Living Room with the flashlight. Perhaps he took her off of Alec with his strong hands. It could have happened. He could have carried her out of the woods, calling for help, with her heavy and lifeless in his arms.

Abby cannot go back to sleep and she cannot call Jenna. She does not know what to do with herself. She wants to watch some kind of movie where she is a character. If she could have the night back that way, it would be fine too. As long as she can have something, instead of this empty space.

The night has no color—it is nothing at all. It is not slept through; it is just not there.

Abby hears a whistle blow. She pictures Chess, on the field, suddenly stopping and looking up at the stands and not seeing her. She changes into jeans (Where did her lucky ones go? She is afraid to ask) and a sweatshirt. She tiptoes down the stairs and gets her army jacket, quietly, and goes out the back door.

The cheers from the school are especially loud. She walks toward them, through the neighbors' lawns and into the woods to the tackling dummies.

She can see the boys, see Chess (#14) running toward the goal, trying to get away from someone, get across a line, trying not to fall down in the process.

She watches him and wonders if he will ever talk to her again. She thinks of his secret, safe inside her ribcage, deeper than that even, all sewn up inside, tight. She watches him run around with hers inside. It's like a tiny story she can picture, playing in his stomach. It is the scene of her mother on a bed, incoherent, all locked up beneath his football padding.

She can see the red and white checked tablecloth clad MADD table, stacked with brownies. She is hungry. She wonders if her stomach is completely empty, if the pump was like a vacuum, if it would have hurt if she had been there.

She wishes she could get a brownie.

She lights a cigarette and watches the ref make a "T" with his hands. She watches as the boys run off to the sidelines. Chess sits down on the bench and takes off his helmet. His hair is sweaty on his head.

Abby watches Chess drink water through a sippy bottle. She thinks of her mother saying "You almost died" and thinks of the game playing on, just like this, with her dead.

Abby looks into the stands and sees Jenna in her black bomber jacket with the shiny pink lining. How can that be? There are Jenna and Alec, sitting next to each other, talking. There are a few other girls around, girls that never talk to Jenna, talking to her. Jenna is using her hands more than usual while she talks. She is laughing. Her hospital bracelet is still on.

Abby is glad she is army green. She is camouflage. It is like she is not there.

She watches as Jenna nudges Alec. She takes out her phone and texts Jenna:

I can see you

She sees Jenna reach into her jacket pocket. Jenna takes out her phone and reads the text. She does not show it to Alec. She does not show it to the other girls. It is as if Jenna, bright in the stands, has an outline around her: Abby can see her so clearly; everyone else is a blur.

Abby holds her phone in her hands, watching as Jenna texts back. She feels the vibration and quickly checks.

Urine saw YOU

This is what it says. She watches as Jenna does not look in her direction. She watches as Jenna pokes Alec in his ribs.

Abby feels hot, then cold. She feels dizzy. She squats down and puts her head between her legs like her father told her to do when she felt faint once. She wonders if this is part of the stomach-pump aftermath. Was she not supposed to leave her bed?

Abby feels scared and like she might throw up. She has to leave, quickly. She turns and suddenly the world is too small, the trees that cover her are closing in. It is like she is at the planetarium and she can't get out. Her breaths begin to come out fast—it is hard to breathe.

She lies down on the ground and looks up at the sky; the branches of the trees seem to be getting bigger, then smaller. She blinks fast—she is scared to close her eyes. She cannot breathe, and wishes someone, even Jenna, would come find her and help her because the trees are darkening the whole sky and the sky is like a dome and it is as if she is trapped inside a snow globe with no snow. The world is too small.

35.

Headie hears the word "lucid." She cannot see.

"Is she lucid?" a man's voice says.

"She's not lucid," a woman's voice says.

She likes the word "lucid." She wonders if what they are talking about is what the word sounds like: bright and clean.

If they knew she could hear them talk about her lucidity, would they think she was lucid? Or would she have to be awake, wide-eyed and talking loudly, for them to consider it?

Someone is holding her hand gently.

"Mother?" another voice says. It is Jeffrey, not Allen. She is not dead.

"Mother?" he says again, but she cannot answer and tell him she is here.

When he was small he was too needy. Sometimes she worried he was too attached. As much as there were problems with Livia, she could tell, at least at first, that having a woman made her son strong.

Livia had been a strong girl in the beginning too. But she had changed. Headie can remember there was a point, on a visit, that she suddenly seemed weaker. She seemed to stop challenging Allen. She spent most of her time in the guest bedroom.

Then there was the way she seemed after she tried to kill herself. In a way it seemed that after that, Jeffrey became even more of a man. His adult self erased his child self. Every time they came to visit, Headie was nervous. She did not know what to expect.

Headie always looked forward to seeing Abby, though. Abby did not seem to change. She was so different from her mother. When Abby hugged her she seemed to give herself completely over, almost knocking Headie backward. When Headie hugged Livia it seemed that her daughter-in-law didn't want to be touched.

Still, Headie knows that Livia is not really weak. She knows what happens with men. A man's job is to be strong; a woman's is to keep his secrets.

Headie was good at that with both of her husbands. It made her a good wife. It was the reason, probably, that neither man left her. She was sure they both cheated (all men cheat), but she had not said anything (even when she knew) and she had let them think that she didn't know. She had cleaned and tied their ties and wiped the shaving cream from their faces when there was some they hadn't washed off. In public she had bragged about her husbands and when she was with them she stood straight and tall with her arm hooked into theirs. She had never said no and she had never yelled and she had watched them see her and she had been what she knew they wanted to see. And it all came naturally.

Headie knew that Livia was not the same way, but she knew that she was bright. So perhaps behind the scenes things were not at all what they looked like from the outside. Perhaps Livia had always been strong, but she had learned to be a wife later, and became less strong-*seeming* to make Jeffrey more so.

"Mother," she hears.

She tries to open her mouth but cannot speak. She feels fine with not being able to, until she hears him again and thinks of it. She will need to tell him. Someone will have to tell him.

Headie likes Livia when she thinks this. It will be Livia who breaks the news to Jeffrey because she can handle it. Jeffrey can lean on her and she will not tell anyone she has seen him cry.

Headie wants her computer. She wants to be able to tell them to get it. Someone could type for her. Maybe she could whisper the words.

Dear Livia, she would say, *I am writing to you so that you can let your husband know. I think you should tell him. I am hardly lucid and you are his wife and will have to deal with whatever happens.*

Headie thinks about how to word what comes next. It is strange how she cannot think of how to say this. For so long what to say had been in her mouth, almost on her lips. For so long she thought she might just blurt it out. But that doesn't seem right now. It must be gentle.

When Allen was still married to his old wife, and I was young, before I met Gene, I got pregnant. Then I moved and did not see Allen for a very long time and I met Gene right after and I married him right then and I had Jeffrey. But Gene is not really Jeffrey's father. Allen is really Jeffrey's father.

This is the way to say it, she thinks. Finally. Livia will read it and think of an even better way. She was an English major, and she is smart. She will be able to do it gently. She was always a sensitive girl.

Perhaps you are thinking I am a bad mother because I never told him or you. There were many times I thought I might tell you but then I did not because you and Jeffrey hated Allen. Another thing is that Allen never knew either.

I feel glad that I am telling you this now because I know you are the best person to tell Jeffrey and I know you will know how to say it right. It will be OK. And Gene was a good father and also never knew and loved Jeffrey as you know.

Love,
Headie

She wants to open her mouth and begin her dictation.

"Mother?" she hears.

Her son's is the only voice in the room.

36.

To: simonepsych@aol.com
From: livia@liviathedesigner.com

Dear Simone—
I am writing to let you know that I will be out of com-
mission for a while. We've had two family emergencies and
my attention is needed. I would still love to work with you,
but it will take some time. I understand if you are in a rush
and therefore need to work with someone else, but I wanted
to let you know that I would be happy to continue with you
when things subside.
Please pass this on to Gail as well.
All the best,
Livia

Livia re-reads the email twice and presses "send." It
is the strangest thing, she thinks, the way motherhood
stops you and relieves you both.

She leans back in her bed. She is tired, but does not
want to sleep. Perhaps she should call Simone, tell her
as well.

She picks up the phone and dials SIMONES but it
goes straight to voicemail so she hangs up; she tries SI-
MONES HOME but no one answers either. She won-

ders if they would have kept her without references or a portfolio. She wonders what it will be like if she sees Simone somewhere in town.

She thinks how she will act confident. She will not go into what happened to Abby. She will tell her that there have been some "family problems" but that they are all worked out now, everything is fine, she is just on hiatus.

Then she will hug Simone and they will kiss on the cheek. Perhaps Simone will be sad that it didn't work out and walk away, regretful, going home to Gail and confessing that she wished they had not scared Livia away, since maybe it was Gail's fault, for intimidating her the way she has of doing.

They will fight. Simone will go for a walk on the beach alone. She will look out at the bay and think that she should call Livia, just to tell her, again, how sorry she is, how it was really Gail's fault, how if it had been up to her . . .

Eventually Simone and Gail will make up, make love in some new bed another designer has chosen. They will lick each other in their mauve room. When they are finished they will lie back and stare at their mauve walls. Secretly, Simone will regret them.

Livia sits up again with her laptop. She thinks she hears Abby, but then realizes the sounds are coming from downstairs, from Jorgen. Perhaps Abby is sleeping. She listens carefully but does not hear her.

Maybe she should call Simone for a therapist for Abby. She thinks of calling Dr. Courtenay. He had called her many times after she stopped going, leaving messages to tell her how important her "treatment" was. The words he used annoyed her: treatment, diagnosis, fantasy. Each of these words had a different meaning in his office. In therapy old words were given new definitions. A fantasy, for example, did not have to be a good thing.

Apparently, Livia's fantasies were angry. Her dreams, apparently, said so. Livia was angry so she slept and ate and tried to kill herself. Her rebellion had not soothed her; she never got the love she needed from her parents.

She would be talking, telling him she thought one thing, and he would change it around, relate it to something else. It was as if everything she did was connected to one long string, and it didn't matter what had happened to her since the string began. It was as if each thing she said pulled her backward. It was exhausting.

She wonders if that is what it would be like for Abby. She certainly won't blame her father. That's a given. Abby sees her father the way Livia used to see Jeffrey: a calmer.

Jeffrey had been smitten by Abby from the day she was born. Livia remembers watching him hold her. On her first birthday she had dressed Abby up and put matching party hats on both her and her daughter, ready with a cake when he got home from work. He began to cry when he saw them, immediately picking Abby up and putting her to his cheek, kissing her forehead.

Livia remembers how it felt each evening, then: as if he came home and swept the day away. He took all of the things that she and Abby had done (or not done) and made them seem very far away, or never there at all.

As she got older, she watched Abby's face change when she heard the door. After a while she would call her father herself instead of asking Livia *When will Dad be home?*

Livia would be the one to blame for everything. On the string of Abby's life, Livia would pull her backwards. It would be a rope in her case, and that rope would be tied around Livia's waist. Perhaps each movement Livia made, Abby would feel. Perhaps the doctor would tell her so.

Livia will not ask Dr. Courtenay. He will recommend someone like him, someone who will make Abby hate her. They will make her see her own anger. They will turn her black inside.

There is a knock on the door. Livia sits up in the bed. It is Jorgen, asking to come in to get the laundry.

"Sure," she says. "Come in."

Jorgen enters and goes straight for her laundry basket, not looking up at her.

She watches him as he pours her basket into the larger basket he is holding. He stands up, suddenly, straight, and looks at her.

"Are you OK, Livia?" he says.

"Of course, Jorgen," she says, looking away from him, down at her computer.

"I think Abby will be good," he says.

"Yes," she says. "I know that, Jorgen."

"Do you want a special dinner?" Jorgen asks.

Why would she want a special dinner?

"Sure," she says. "Make whatever you want."

"Great!" Jorgen says, turning around to go make his special dinner. He closes the door behind him.

Is she OK? She is not sure. She does not want a psychiatrist to tell her. She wants Abby to be better. She is like Jorgen that way, she thinks, then smiles, then feels like she might cry again.

Is she OK? She does not know.

She picks up the phone and calls SIMONES again who picks up and tells her that she was just going to call her back since she saw her name on the missed calls list.

"Do you think," Livia asks, "I can come by and talk to you about my daughter?"

37.

Headie can hear it but it doesn't sound real. It sounds like a dog or a cartoon baby.

She can feel it too. He is shaking. He has put her hand to his face and his face is wet. He is not saying anything to her, just crying. Her only son.

There is something in her nose; it feels like a tube. It is new, uncomfortable, she realizes now, as she tries to move her lips. Her mouth is dry.

She cannot open her eyes, but she can breathe. It feels so easy, breathing. It is as if she is outside, in the fall, walking around the way she used to, sometimes just around the block, sometimes to the post office if she had letters.

She knew there was something wrong with email. It makes you stay at home. It made her unplug her phone and live on the floor. It made her not want to ever leave.

When she gets home she won't email as much, she thinks. Still, it was nice. It was easier than a phone call. It was so quick—it is still hard to believe.

"Mom," she can hear her son say again.

What does he want her to do? She is trying, she wants to tell him. She at least would like to tell him that.

She has always been trying, she wants to tell him. That is all. Isn't that what parents are supposed to do? Try their best.

I've tried my best at everything, she thinks.

It's true: sometimes Allen yelled. She did not talk about it, and she did not yell back. She liked when he came home at night, expecting a meal. She liked the way he watched cartoons in the morning, laughing at them, while she served him breakfast.

At dinner, sometimes, they would eat in silence. They ate in the dining room at opposite ends of the table, far away. She did not try to make conversation if he did not start it. She liked to hear him chewing, sometimes making a noise to tell her he was enjoying what she had made.

They watched TV together in bed before they went to sleep. Allen liked funny sitcoms, and Headie would lie next to him, watching, until he fell asleep. Then she would pull the covers around him and tuck them, close, the way he liked, like a mummy, and turn off the TV. She would look at his face, sometimes, because it was the only time she could get so close. She would kiss him softly on the cheek three times, for good luck.

Sometimes Headie wondered what his old wife had done. Headie knew she was nowhere near as beautiful as his ex-wife, and that beauty was not the reason he was with her. She knew that there were a few reasons: one was the sex (especially in the beginning) and the other was that she was who he wanted her to be.

She had thought about it once, thought about saying it. It was on their honeymoon in Greece, in the beginning. She had not yet figured the exact shape that he wanted her to be; there was some leeway then, and she thought she might be able to stick some things in.

And vacations made things forgivable, she thought. She had never been anywhere like Greece. It was white and blue and so bright she wore sunglasses in their hotel room because the sun shone in. It felt like a dream, being there with him.

In the beginning, he was not cruel. He was not even irritable until a few months later. She remembers the day it began: he was looking at the grocery bills. Apparently she had spent too much. He called her stupid.

In the beginning, they sat on a beach in Greece. They held hands and moved their fingers between each other's in the sand.

Headie wore a hat, she remembers. She felt confident in hats. They made her face look almost heart-shaped. They took away the smallness of her forehead and let people guess how far her hairline went.

On the beach, she watched the young girls without their bikini tops. She watched the young men, all muscles and dark sweat. Everything felt sexy and good, and every day they went back to their room and made love before dinner.

They were sitting in the sand and holding hands and Headie looked at a couple, young and holding hands too, sitting in front of them. She thought of her son and Livia, back in New York. She had written them a postcard the day before, telling them she was having a good time, not to worry, it was beautiful, and love. She wrote: *PS—I will be home soon.* The day before, she and Allen had walked to the post office (even the post office was white!) and put it in the mail.

The young couple lay back on their towel and began kissing. Headie couldn't stop watching (months later, Allen would get angry about her staring, and would get mad at her when they went to a restaurant and he caught her looking at people) but then he said nothing, and she watched, looking forward to going back to the room.

Soon the couple got up (the man adjusted himself; Headie did not look away) and left the beach. Headie looked at her new husband.

Sometimes she thought how oblivious everyone was. How could they not tell? Looking at Allen's profile, thinking of her son: same blue eyes, same bump on the nose, same leanness and eyebrows. How could everyone be so stupid?

But no one ever said anything. It was true: Gene wasn't fat or short. She could see how it could be. And there was a little bit of her there, too, she knew, in the shape of his mouth, the shape of his teeth.

She looked at her new husband, watching the waves. Sometimes it still seemed unreal to her: Mrs. Headra Goldstein. She had been a Mrs. for a long time, but this was different. She was no longer married to a dead man. Her husband was there, next to her, thinking thoughts, looking out at the sea.

He never commented on Jeffrey, only on "the girl," Livia, and her smart-ass ways. Headie listened but did not say anything.

Perhaps he knew not to say anything about Jeffrey. Headie talked to her son, still, once a week. When she got off the phone, sometimes Allen would ask her what

Jeffrey had said. She would tell him—he seemed to lis-ten—but he would not say anything back.

Headie wondered if Allen had ever wanted chil-dren. Later, on another vacation (this time to San Fran-cisco), he would tell her he had. Vacations were always good for them that way. They talked more.

Back then, though, she was not sure. Still, watching him, the way the sun was shining, the way he looked so much like Jeffrey sitting like that, perhaps the rosy lenses of her glasses made it seem inevitable.

"Allen," she said, pulling his hand up from the sand, taking it in both of hers.

"What?" he said. He turned away from the sea and seemed to be remembering she was there. He looked at her.

Suddenly there was a shadow: a man selling jewelry came to sit in front of them. He laid out a big black case with beautiful aqua-blue beads made into necklaces and bracelets. Some of them were painted with little eyes.

"Evil eye," the man said pointing to them.

The man looked like he had come out of the sea, sunburned and tattered. Headie looked at his beads, picked up a necklace.

"We'll take that," Allen said, reaching for his wallet in Headie's bag where he had told her to keep it behind her. Later she would teach him how to search in a woman's bag: don't use your eyes, just feel for the shape of what you are looking for.

Headie kept looking at the jewelry. She wasn't sure that she wanted that one—that necklace: there were so many. She spotted one she liked better. It had more eyes on it.

She began to put the first one down and to pick up the other when Allen said, "Where the fuck is my wallet, Headie?"

It was gone, stolen. That was that. The honeymoon, her chance, had been ruined.

Headie feels her son, still, and then feels him gone. Suddenly her hand is cold. She had stopped thinking about him touching it, and now she wishes he was back—where did he go?—keeping it warm.

She concentrates and hears what must be the TV. Suddenly: a song. Suddenly: the dancers.

There they are. Coming this time as if from behind a black curtain, coming out on a stage for an encore. There is a woman in the middle, spinning around and around. She is in pink. Headie can't see her face.

The two men on her sides are Headie's husbands. They are doing the same dance, but Allen looks silly, like someone is making his feet move that way, without his permission.

Gene looks handsome in a way that she never thought he was. He dances so well. He stops the woman from spinning so that she freezes, standing with her back to the audience. Allen turns her around.

There she is, the first wife, the shiksa, looking the way she did when Allen first brought her home. She is young and so beautiful, it is hard to believe. Headie thinks of her and how she probably never thought of Headie. She had never spoken to her, not once.

The shiksa is red-lipped, gorgeous. She blows kisses and a bouquet of red roses magically appears in Allen's hands. He gives them to her as she curtsies. The curtain begins to close.

38.

Abby hears the game from the ground. It is as loud as it was before. She stands up slowly and looks back at the bleachers. Everyone—Jenna—is still there, all in the same places. She looks down at her feet, her unlucky jeans. She is in the woods, as if nothing has happened.

She had been lying there, and then nothing. Different than before, but still. She can breathe better, but she is scared in a new way now. She is scared it will happen again.

She gets up, looking quickly (she can't help it) back at the field, back at Jenna. She has the urge to wave. She has the urge to walk through the field and punch her.

Instead she turns, runs back through the neighbors' lawns, relieved she no longer feels faint, no longer feels nauseous. She runs quickly, like someone is chasing her, like if she doesn't move fast enough she will feel that way again. She runs to the back door of her house and opens it.

Jorgen is standing in the kitchen, looking like he has been caught doing something wrong. He is holding something behind him.

"Hi," she says, walking past him. She does not look him in the eye. She does not want to think about what he saw.

"I'm making a special dinner," he says, calling after her as she walks through the dining room, runs up the stairs.

She shuts her door and takes off all her dirt-stained clothes—they are uncomfortable suddenly—and lies in her bed. She tries to imagine the wheel, spinning, but she cannot. She breathes in squares (in for five, hold for five, out for five, hold for five) the way her mother taught her when she was in her yoga phase.

It's not working. It is as if the breathing makes her heart beat faster. It is as if the breathing is a blanket trying to cover up the heartbeat. It is as if the breathing is a veil over an ugly girl's pounding face.

Abby stops the square breathing. She does not want to go downstairs ever again. She wishes Jorgen would just put her "special dinner" on a tray outside her bedroom door so that she can get it when she is hungry.

It kills her: Jenna. How had she stayed awake? Had Jenna (had everyone?) seen Jorgen? Had they seen her? Her pubic hair?

She can hear someone coming up the stairs. She quickly gets up and puts on her bathrobe. It is her mother, her stomps.

She opens the door before her mother can knock.

"Hi," her mother says, walking in without asking, sitting on Abby's bed.

Her mother looks raw without makeup. Her eyes are still red. Abby wonders if she kept crying after Abby left her in the den.

Abby sits on the floor.

RACHEL SHERMAN

"Abby," her mother says, "the principal called and they are suspending you for two days."

Abby looks at her mother, then at the carpet, wiping her hands against it so that the pile is dark and then light.

"What?" Abby says. "Is Jenna suspended too?" Abby's mother looks strange, surprised.

"I don't know," she says. "They didn't say."

"That's crazy!" Abby says. "I just saw Jenna at the game. She isn't suspended!"

Abby's mother's voice suddenly gets louder.

"At the game? What do you mean?" she says.

"At the homecoming game at school," she says, getting up, walking over to her jewelry box, opening the drawers, not even looking at what's inside (she knows what's there—it is all a shiny blur), then sitting down at her desk. "Can't you hear it?"

"Yes," Livia says, her voice softer now. "I didn't know you left—you aren't supposed to leave."

"Why?" Abby asks. "Because I'm *grounded*?"

Saying this, she has a new tone. She can feel a new feeling. She can see it in her mother's face, see the new feeling leave her and spread across the room.

It is from her body, but has nothing to do with the sexy parts. It is far, far away from those.

This is something new, and she can feel it make her mouth open. She can feel it make her face hot, her arms tense. She has not felt this before, and yet it feels familiar. It feels terrible and wonderful at the same time: the oddest relief.

Abby's mother is looking at her strangely. She can see on her mother's face how it is new to them all.

Abby looks down at her fingernails, waiting for her mother. Does she even know what it means to be grounded? Does her mother know what to do?

"So, am I?" Abby says, pulling her thumbnail cuticle off so it bleeds.

There is silence, and Abby looks up again, at her mother, her face too white around the eyes. There is a definite difference between her (makeup-less) mother and the one that goes out. When she thinks of her mother she is big and loud and sad all over the place. Her mother is running with a snotty tissue, sticking it out for Abby to take away; Livia is big-hipped, smile-lined, full of something that Abby is not always sure of. But now, she sees a difference between the mom she imagines and the mom in front of her, who is small and seems scared.

Still, Abby cannot help it.

"Tell me!" she yells, getting up and going over to her desk, sitting down, scribbling on a piece of paper. Drawing circles, then Christmas trees, then eggs, over easy, again and again.

"I'm going to call your father," Abby's mother says. "You should talk to him. We should see how Bubbe is."

Abby's mother gets up and walks out of the room. Abby walks behind her, then slams the door as soon as she is on the hallway carpet.

She can hear her mother clomping down the stairs, fast, stomping on each stair, as if there is not a path she should take, as if she is drunk, as if the stairs are a different shape that only she can see. Abby always wants to tell her to hold the railing.

Abby will never walk like this. Abby will tiptoe everywhere. When she sneaks out of the house again to meet Chess on her lawn she will be so quiet that no one—not even Jorgen—will hear her.

On the lawn, at night, Chess will light a cigarette. He will be showered from after the game, but still pink-faced from so much running. He will be out of breath, but for no real reason, since the game has been over for hours.

He will smile. He will tell her "no worries." He will tell her no one saw, it wasn't a big deal, it happens all the time.

Jenna is a bitch, he will say, and she will nod into the space inside his armpit where her head fits perfectly. She will smell his deodorant and she will move to his chest. He will kiss her on the forehead.

39.

Livia watches her daughter change shapes, turn colors, switch sounds. She watches Abby move from one side of her room to the other.

She wants to know if she is grounded.

Livia watches her daughter, her hair in her face, her nails bloody, the bruise where the IV was in her arm. Her daughter's voice is hoarse, and she wants to tell her to calm down. But Livia hates when people say this to her, has vowed never to say that to anyone, never to say "too much information" and make someone feel stupid when they've told her maybe a bit too much, and never to say "ugh, huh?" in a way that makes the person that has told you what they have told you suddenly regret it.

People have said all these things to Livia. Also: *Take it down a notch* (that was Jeffrey). It has always seemed crazy to Livia to think that someone could tell someone else how to temper their own feelings. They did not know what was going on, how one thing had led to another which had led to the moment where this was how she felt. For a reason.

Calm down, she thinks, watching Abby.

Livia tries to think of what to say. For the first time, she truly wishes Jeffrey were back. She is not sure that he would know what to say, but he would say something—no words were coming to her at all.

It makes her wonder, watching Abby, if this daughter has been hiding. If this is the daughter she has always had. If this is her daughter, this silent seether, and she had not noticed. She thinks of the beers on the lawn.

"So, am I?" her daughter yells.

Livia wonders if Jorgen can hear her. She feels her face flush and rubs her eyes.

Take it down a notch, she thinks.

She wonders what Jeffrey would do. Would he ignore her, the way he did with Livia when she was like this? Would he comfort Abby the way he used to comfort Livia?

What if Livia took her arms and squeezed her?

She had once seen a TV show where an autistic woman who worked on a farm made a contraption that mimicked the equipment the cows were placed in when they were being held for milking. The plastic was green: the autistic lady (short-haired, looked like a lesbian) lay down on it and the plastic expanded like a blood-pressure cuff to wrap around her, firmly and gently, holding her in place, just like a cow.

Livia often thinks of that and wonders if you can really buy one of those. She could do without sex if she had something like that. If something could squeeze her so tight, and by the feeling, let her know that she is there without being even touched, she might be able to sometimes "control herself."

Perhaps Abby needs one too. Together they could go inside their contraptions, be fed by Jorgen, like cows.

Relax, Livia thinks, putting her hands out in the air as if to stop her daughter, for just a second, from moving back and forth.

Livia thinks: this must be it. This must be what I get. This must be what my father said: I hope you have a girl as bad as you.

Livia looks at her daughter's feet. They are too white, with lines on them where her socks must have been. She wonders about the rest of her daughter's body, what her breasts are like (she is always wearing baggy shirts), and what else, if anything, she got from Livia.

Abby is looking at her, straight in the eyes.

"Tell me!" Abby says.

She has to answer.

She hears Jorgen downstairs.

"I'm going to go down and call your father," Livia says. "You should talk to him. We should see how Bubbe is."

She gets up, passing Abby (she can feel her: a cool breeze and then something hot) and then she smells her: cigarettes and evergreen trees.

She passes by Abby and flinches. It feels like her daughter might hit her.

Instead her daughter slams the door behind her. It shakes the house.

Livia goes downstairs. She leaves her daughter in her room where she cannot escape (except to the roof, and there is no way she can get down from there). She is supposed to call her husband, to ask him what to do. But instead she goes to the kitchen where it smells of meat.

In the kitchen there is a pot steaming. There are carrots cooking. There must be some kind of meat somewhere. There are mashed potatoes.

Livia sits down at the kitchen table. She wants a glass of wine, but she needs to take care of Abby; she knows this. Just until tomorrow or the next day, until she sees Simone, until someone can tell her what to do.

"It is almost ready, Livia," Jorgen says.

Livia does not want to eat with him. She goes into her bedroom, closes the door, and calls Jeffrey.

"She woke up!" he says as soon as he picks up the phone. "She's not talking yet, but she blinks to let me know that she understands."

"That's great. I'm so glad. Please kiss her for me." Livia pauses. "Abby wants to know if she's grounded."

"Um, yes, I think that's a good idea. Yes. She's grounded."

"So I have to tell her she can't go anywhere?" Livia asks.

"Yes, Liv," he says in his old voice, as if she is stupid. "She can't leave at all."

Livia hangs up and takes out her storage bin. She takes out her chips, opens a new can of dip, and sits on the floor. She puts the news station on the TV and begins. She cannot eat fast enough.

Someone knocks on the door and Livia grabs her bag. The door opens quickly; Livia has potato chips in her mouth. She is mid-scoop.

It is her daughter. She has changed out of her bathrobe into one of her big flannel shirts and jeans. Abby walks over to where she is sitting on the floor. Livia chews and swallows.

Livia does not look up. She does not want to see her daughter's eyes.

When her daughter turns, she realizes that she has not moved. Her chip is still in her hand, as if she is paralyzed.

"Fucking pigpen," she hears her daughter whisper, slamming the door again.

40.

Headie feels like she has just woken up but she does not remember falling asleep. It is as if suddenly she can hear things, even though her eyes are still closed. No one is touching her, but she hears Jeffrey breathing.

"Fuck!" she hears her son say, probably to no one. Maybe to her. She has never known him to be a swearer.

She is no swearer. She is no yeller or whiner either. Still, she wishes she could talk. If only she could open her eyes.

She wonders what is wrong.

She hears her son sigh again.

The door opens. "Hello, Mr. Schecter." It is a woman's voice.

"Mrs. Goldstein," she says. "Can you hear me?" She feels her eyelid being lifted and sees an Oriental lady's eyes squint back at her. She can feel the lady's cold fingers holding her eyelids up.

If only I could talk with my eyeballs, she thinks.

The Oriental lets go, but Headie can still see out of the eye that was lifted.

"Look," she says, "her eye's still open."

Headie can see her son come up close.

"Mom?" he says, his voice starting to get sniffly again.

Headie tries to move her eyes as much as she can.

"It looks like she's awake." The woman is fat for an Oriental.

Jeffrey sits on the edge of the bed; he holds a straw up to her lips and she drinks a sip of water. He looks tired.

"There you go, Mrs. Goldstein," the nurse says. It is starting to bother her, the way the nurse talks to her. Calling her Mrs. but acting as if she is a child.

Headie clears her throat. She looks at her son.

"Do you understand me, Mom? Blink once if you do," he says.

Headie blinks—not to say "Yes," although she does understand—but because her eyes are dry.

"Oh, Mom," he says, leaning forward and kissing her cheek, her forehead, her other cheek.

Headie does not say anything. She is sure that if she wanted to, she would be able to speak. But she feels tired and calm. Perhaps they are giving her medication to make her feel this way. Perhaps, really, she is in pain.

Jeffrey's phone rings and he looks at it, then holds out his finger to tell her it will only be a minute.

"It's Liv," he says to her. Then, into the phone, "She woke up! She's not talking yet, but she blinks to let me know that she understands."

Headie watches her son talk. He picks at his cuticles (just like his father). She hears him say "Abby" and "grounded." His face changes; he seems angry. "Yes, Liv," he says. "She can't leave at all."

Grounded. Headie never had to ground her son. He probably read about that in parenting books.

Why would they ground that sweet girl? The last time she saw Abby, last April when they came to visit, she looked more like a young lady. It was hard to see her figure—she covered it up—but you could tell she was thin. Her hair was in her face, so Headie pushed it behind her ear while they were watching TV. Abby didn't stop her. She turned to her and smiled.

"You have such nice skin," Headie told her granddaughter. She patted the back of her head.

She watched her granddaughter watch the television. She thought about how she would make creamed herring in the morning and Jeffrey would eat it. She would make chopped liver that night for an hors d'oeuvre. She would make her famous potato salad (the only thing that Abby and Livia seemed to eat at her house).

Her granddaughter was quiet, mostly, speaking only when spoken to. She leaned her head on her father sometimes—Headie knew how that was. She had loved her father like that too.

Headie watches her son hang up his phone and come back to her, suddenly focused again.

"Mom," he says. "I love you."

Headie knows this. It is enough, and she does not even mouth the words. She is tired, but not sleepy.

Everyone around her will stay. She does not have to move. It is the best feeling she has had in a long time. She watches her son smile.

She wonders if other people have felt this kind of calm. Is she actually dying? Or is it that she just does not feel like doing living things?

Other people think she is dying. Headie wonders if everyone believes one thing but you do not, does that makes it true? Because inside, Headie feels alive. She feels like dancing.

Headie feels her eyes closing again.

"Mom?" she hears.

Then she hears music, something old, and there are her men, and there are some women. There is Gene doing flips. There is Allen swaying. There is her sister being flipped by someone she can't see.

There is Abby, dancing fast, holding her mother's hands. Livia moves her feet with her daughter. They are wearing matching green dresses.

Headie wants to join in. She is not a good dancer, but some of the other people are not that great either.

She feels badly for Allen, swaying in the corner, but it is Livia and Abby she wants to join in with.

She feels her eyes close. She can hear music and breathing. She cannot feel anything physical, but the stage is bright in front of her.

Someone is pointing. It is Allen—no, Gene. It is only the dead people now, dancing in a circle, like the hora. They have Allen up in a chair. They have her father there too.

Suddenly she is being lifted. She can see them dancing all around. She is up in the chair, then she is down, and then she is moving, her feet doing things she did not know they could do. Dancing, dancing, dancing.

41.

"Special dinner!" she can hear Jorgen call from downstairs.

"I'm not hungry," Abby yells back down. She is lying on her bed, her eyes closed, thinking of her mother.

"But it's good for you. Meat and potatoes."

"I'm not hungry," she says again. She gets up and turns on the radio to the top forty station, then lies back down again. Her mother can eat Jorgen's dinner. She will be happy to eat it. She was hungry, wasn't she? Abby thinks of her: piggy, stuffing her face.

There is a knock on the door (no preceding footsteps; was the music that loud?). Abby gets out of bed, turns down the radio, and goes to the door.

Jorgen stands on the other side of the brass bar of her carpet. He is holding a tray with food. It smells good.

"You have to get healthy," he says. "You have to eat."

"Thank you, Jorgen, but really, I'm not hungry."

She cannot look at him. She has to look at his sandaled feet. She remembers how one fell off while he and Jenna were on the kitchen floor. How the bottom of his sock was bright white.

"But it's good for you," he says.

She can feel him trying to get her to look at him. She feels like he can see inside her. He is like the blackness—all the time that she missed. If she looks inside of Jorgen, she thinks, she can find her missing hours.

She wishes he would die.

"Fine," she says. It is the only way to get him to leave. She takes the tray into her room and shuts the door.

She puts the tray on the floor and looks down at the food. She wonders if her mother always ate the way she saw her in her room. Her fucking piggy self. It made Abby want to throw water on her for some reason. To drench her in something.

What was the point of any dinner? Abby thinks. Her mother hardly ever eats and when she does she only eats healthy and plain. Now she knows why.

It makes sense. How could she not have thought of it before? Someone who ate nothing would be skinny. Her mother is not skinny. She actually looks healthy, which is even stranger.

She wonders if her father knows. If she is now in on a secret that was just between them. Or if he has no idea. Perhaps she has a secret of her own.

Abby looks at the dinner. It is still steaming. It is meatballs and potatoes, things her mother never has Jorgen cook.

Abby opens her window, looking out at where she is not allowed to be. She can't remember when the cheering stopped. The game is long over.

She gets her cigarettes from her closet and climbs out the window. She is not worried about getting caught.

What will her mother do? What can anyone do now that she is already grounded?

She smokes two cigarettes, then goes back inside and touches a meatball with her finger. They are still a bit warm.

She takes the fork from the left (one of the first things her mother showed Jorgen was how to set the table properly) and the knife from the right and begins to eat.

The potatoes are mashed and buttered and perfect. She hates to think about food this way, but it is true. They are perfect potatoes that fall perfectly into her stomach. She eats.

She feels warm inside. She wants seconds. The heat in the house is hardly on. She decides to turn it up.

She goes into the hallway and puts the thermostat way up, then goes back into her room. She wants to feel hot both inside and out.

She wants more potatoes. She leaves her room and brings her tray downstairs. Jorgen is sitting at the dining room table alone, his food out—with the places for herself and her mother set.

"Hello," he says, waving from the table. "Did you like it?"

Abby nods, sits down at her place at the table across from Jorgen and puts down her tray in front of her. She fills up her plate with seconds and puts the plate on the tray. She begins to eat, just a bite before she goes back upstairs, but then she keeps eating, not looking up at Jorgen, not going anywhere.

"Abby, you scared everybody," Jorgen says.

Abby doesn't look up at him. She continues to eat her potatoes. She doesn't want to ask him anything.

"I found you out there," he says.

She takes more meatballs. They are just as good.

"I carried you out," he says.

Abby is eating fast. The meatballs are small, but she can't stop.

"Do you want to know?" Jorgen says.

She hates him and wishes he would shut up and just cook like this every day. Keep her warm, save her.

Her eyes begin to tear up, but she does not wipe them. Perhaps he will not notice if she just keeps eating.

"I won't tell," he says.

There are tears in her mashed potatoes but she cleans her plate.

42.

Livia prints out her dreams. She only prints them out from the past two months, since they are daily, so many, and too much.

She prints out her dreams just in case. Perhaps there is a clue.

Today is a new day. She writes her dream from the night before: (*fires, a man (Jeffrey?) inside some kind of castle . . . dreading feeling, as if there is someone behind each door that I do not know about. Abby somewhere in the castle (with Jeffrey?) vague . . . unknown*), showers, dresses (the good black slacks, turquoise shirt), puts on her heels and walks down to the basement.

Jorgen is standing outside his bedroom door.

"I heard you," he says. He looks like he has been up since dawn, his hair parted on the side, his eyes bright, awake.

"Oh," Livia says, brushing back her hair. "I'm just coming down to tell you that Abby is grounded. Do you know what that means?"

"No," Jorgen says. "I do not."

"That means that she cannot leave the house under *any* circumstances. I am going out to a doctor's appointment, but it is your job to make sure she doesn't leave."

"Oh," Jorgen says. "I made food she can eat for lunch."

"OK," Livia says, "but do you understand? No matter what. She can't leave."

"Yes, I understand," Jorgen says.

"Great," Livia says, turning around to walk back upstairs. She can hear Jorgen following behind her.

Livia does not tell Abby she is leaving. She does not want to go upstairs, and besides, if Abby knows that she is gone she might try to sneak out.

Livia takes her printouts, her onion dip and chips, and pulls out of the driveway. She drives through town and then out to the Neck. The leaves are so beautiful now, but it is already getting chilly. Looking at the leaves, she thinks of Abby. It occurs to her, suddenly, that she must have been cold when they found her.

Livia thinks of her daughter's face, her disgust. She had forgotten about the pigpen—she had not thought of it in years. Thinking of what she must have looked like to Abby makes her want to die.

Livia drives across the Causeway and turns the heat up in the car. It is gray out, and the water looks rough. Usually Livia thinks of herself as a person who likes the fall. It reminds her of getting back-to-school outfits with her mother. Her mother always came into the stall to watch her try things on.

Livia turns in to Simone's driveway. She can see from outside that there are tan curtains hung in the living room, and rice-paper shades in the bedroom. She thinks about what people would say if she told them about the pigpen.

There is Simone's Volvo and a Jeep in the driveway. Livia hopes that Gail is not home. She hates the thought of having to go into a room with Simone and close the door, like having an actual session. She wants this to be easy: they can sit in the living room and drink wine like friends.

The door opens and a tall brown-haired boy wearing a white button-down and khaki shorts answers the door. He smiles and she sees. It is Abby's friend: Chess.

Chess stops smiling.

"How is Abby?" he asks, crossing his legs and standing in the doorway, his arm against one side, seemingly keeping her out. He seems calm and not surprised to see her.

"She's fine," Livia says. She feels embarrassed but she is not sure why. She wonders if Abby knows what she knows.

"I didn't know about it. I mean, I wasn't there, really," he starts to speak.

"I'm here to see Simone," she says, stopping him. She does not mean to be rude—it just comes out that way.

Chess looks her in the eye. He is so handsome. She does not want him to talk. He is the kind of boy Livia would have loved if she were Abby.

"Simone!" he calls, turning, up the stairs. He walks away, leaving the door open. Livia steps inside.

"Coming!" she can hear Simone yell down.

Livia stands in the front hall but peeks into the living room. Still no paint. No new furniture. Just the curtains. Livia is relieved.

"Hello!" Simone says, seeming happy to see her, walking down the stairs. She is wearing jeans and a long-sleeved shirt. Her hair is swept to the side in a barrette.

"Did you meet Chess?" Simone asks. "Gail's son," she says, walking into the living room. Livia begins to follow her. She looks down at Simone's bare feet.

"Oh, sorry!" Livia says, taking off her shoes.

"Oh, no no," Simone says, sitting on the couch and putting her legs beneath her, "they're starting to redo the floors tomorrow. It really doesn't matter."

Livia stops slipping off her shoes and walks into the living room. There are pictures out now, and only a few boxes pushed against the wall. Next to her: a picture of Chess, younger, graduating from something, smiling, in between Gail and Simone.

"You've been unpacking," Livia says.

"Yes, yes," says Simone. "I devoted all day yesterday to finally living here."

"Oh wait," says Simone, "do you want something to drink? I have a nice Chardonnay . . ."

"Sure," Livia says, and Simone goes into the kitchen. Livia can hear Chess's footsteps. She wonders if he is calling Abby to tell her that her mother is there. For some reason it feels wrong that he is home. Or maybe that she is in his house. She wishes he would leave.

Simone brings in the glasses and sits back down.

"So," she says. "You're having some problems with your daughter?"

Livia realizes that Simone does not know. Chess has not told her. Her daughter, in this house, will be made up of her words. She must be careful, she realizes. To Simone, her daughter is new.

She relays the story, taking sips throughout. Simone nods her head, says "Hmmm, hmmmm," looking concerned. It makes Livia feel good, the way Simone's brows furrow, showing her that what is happening is hard; she is not feeling sorry for herself.

"So, she's at home now?" Simone says.

"Yes," Livia says. "She's grounded."

"Huh," Simone says, getting up. "I'm just going to get more wine," she says, walking into the kitchen.

Livia likes the way Simone drinks: unguiltily. Each move she makes is as if it was the exact move that was supposed to be made. It seems like Simone was born a woman—like she was never a girl.

"And now she's suspended for two days, and my husband is away—his mother fell the day this happened."

"Oh my God," Simone says. "That's terrible. It must have been horrifying to see your daughter in the hospital, all alone."

"It was," Livia says and then begins to cry. It is so good to hear Simone say things, so validating. Livia remembers when she had mentioned therapy to Jeffrey before she took the pills. He said that therapists were just people you paid to agree with you.

Livia isn't paying, though. Simone is her friend.

"Yeah, so, it's just been hard. But mostly I'm just worried about Abby. I can't tell you how different she is acting."

"How is that?" Simone asks.

"Yelling, cursing," Livia says.

"And how old is she?" Simone asks.

"Fifteen," Livia says.

Simone smiles.

"Well, I'm sure she's humiliated. I mean, think of it. And you also have to remember that she is right in the middle of adolescence. Acting out is the norm."

Livia wonders if Chess acts out. She knew boys like him when she was young. They were not always as sweet as they seemed.

Maybe Chess was mad that his mother was a lesbian. Does Abby know?

"Really," Simone says. "Her behavior is nothing unusual—I mean, her anger. What has happened, though, is a real cry for help. I have a great referral for you. Usually adolescent girls prefer to go to women."

Livia thinks about telling her how in their family, it's not like that. In their family, Abby does not seem at all interested in speaking to women. Or at least not to her. In their family Abby is bonded to her father. It was why she had the idea to hire Jorgen in the first place. Abby is more comfortable with men.

"Thank you," Livia says. "Thank you so much for listening."

Simone gets up and Livia feels a wave of panic. She still wants to show her the dreams. She does not want to leave: she wants another glass of wine, to share a cigarette on the porch, to kiss Simone or Chess, to take them upstairs to one of their white, white bedrooms.

Livia watches as Simone walks across the room and leans over the couch Livia is sitting on to straighten a picture above her. Livia had not noticed the picture before, and as she watches Simone (Simone stretching above her to touch the frame, her midriff bared, her stomach tight, toned) she sees past her, to the door. Chess is standing in it, watching.

Livia is worried—what if he has heard her? What if he knows now . . . but what is she afraid that he knows? She has not yet taken out her dreams. He only knows that she is a bad mother. And boys don't care about that.

"Simone," he says. "When is my mom getting home?"

Simone stands back from the picture and Livia watches as she closes one eye and then the other, staring at the frame.

"Soon, I think," Simone says, then turns to Chess, focused. "Do you need something, honey?" she asks.

"No, that's OK," he says, smiling, turning, walking back up the stairs in bare feet.

Simone walks into the kitchen again and asks Livia if she wants another drink. Livia says yes and listens to both Simone's and Chess's footsteps.

Livia's dreams are in her bag, but she is consumed with Chess. She wonders if this is the way whole families are, families everywhere, walking in and out of rooms so calmly, moving as if everyone should want to be in their bodies. Saying simple things like "Do you know?" and "Do you need?" walking around their houses barefoot.

She can still hear Simone's voice saying *honey, honey, honey.*

Simone walks back in and pours her another glass. It is her third now, and after the first few sips, she feels it. She wonders if Simone feels it too, or if this is just the way she is, drinking wine, sipping, straightening frames. Perhaps this is normal, relaxing at home.

Abby does not move around their house the way Chess does, lazily, smiling, crossing from one room to another. Livia wonders if this is her fault. Perhaps Abby has been imitating her. She has never liked their house. She has always missed Philadelphia.

Simone comes back and pours Livia more wine. Livia looks up at her.

"I've brought some of my dreams—I type them up—maybe you could look at them?" she says.

Simone goes back to her chair and sits Indian style.

"Oh," she says. "That would probably be better for you to do with your own therapist. Are you in treatment?"

She says this so casually. She smiles—she is not trying to be mean.

No, Livia wants to say, I want YOU to read them.

"Oh, no, I just thought . . ."

"I can give you a great referral," Simone says.

Livia does not want to share her dreams with anyone else. She wants to give them to Simone, hand over the whole stack, and have her sort through.

"No, no, that's OK," Livia says. She looks in the doorway to make sure that Chess did not hear her getting rejected. She is embarrassed. This is not what she meant.

What Livia meant was to say: Here, take these, I am done with them. I don't know what to do with them—they only make so much sense.

Here Simone, she meant to say, because I can no longer stand myself. Because I go to sleep to escape but dream so vividly that it is like I never rest.

Here you go, Simone, Livia meant to say, because I'm damned both ways. If I don't dream I will die.

Livia says nothing. She looks out the window. She wants to go back in her car, back to her dip, back to her home.

Instead she begins to cry.

"Oh, Livia, honey," Simone says, getting up and walking over to the couch, sitting beside her, putting her small arm around her shoulders.

"I know it's hard," Simone says, and Livia leans into her boney chest. She feels too big, like she can't fit right, like she will knock Simone backwards on the couch.

Simone smells clean. She can feel her breath in her hair. Simone rubs her back, back and forth, back and forth.

"Oh, honey," Simone says.

Livia turns her face so that it fits into the crook of Simone's neck. Then she puts her wet cheek on Simone's soft, dry one. She moves close and kisses Simone, softly, on the mouth.

Simone kisses back, and Livia holds on to her shoulders. She feels Simone's tongue, her soft lips. Livia feels like she is searching for something; she feels like a man.

Simone tenses up, pushes Livia, gently, back.

"No, no," Simone says, wiping her mouth. "This isn't what you need. I'm sorry," she says, getting up and walking into the kitchen.

Livia wipes her mouth. Her hand is smeared with her own lipstick.

She can hear the water running in the other room, then Simone's footsteps again.

Simone stands in the doorway, all the way across the room.

"I think it would be best if you left, Livia. I would be happy to talk to you about this another day."

Livia wipes her eyes. She feels drunk and tired. She takes out her dreams from her purse and puts them next to her on the couch.

"OK," she says, and walks toward the door. She can hear rock music coming from upstairs.

She opens Simone's front door, walks through it, and closes it behind her. She gets into her car, turns on the heat, and drives away from her dreams.

43.

Abby is still in bed when the phone rings. She is still full from the night before, still tired.

"Abby?" It's her dad. His voice sounds hoarse. "Is Mom there?"

"I don't know," she says.

"Abby, Bubbe died," he says.

Abby sits up.

"She did?" she says.

Only a few days ago they had been emailing. Abby tries to remember what her Bubbe last wrote.

"Yes," he says, in his old gentle voice. "You and Mom will have to drive out."

"What happened?" she asks. She can hear her own voice, still hoarse too.

"She went peacefully, Abby, she wasn't in pain. She loved you very much," he says. She hears his voice crack.

"I'm sorry, Dad," she says.

"I know," Abby's father says. "You'll come here today. I love you."

After they hang up Abby lies back down. She tries to picture her father in the hospital, her Bubbe dead.

Before her other grandmother died, Abby went to see her in the hospital. Her mother's mother looked bloated and strange, tubes everywhere; her blue eyes, halfway open, looked milky.

Abby had been younger, but she remembers her grandmother being propped up in the bed, higher than them, almost as if she was looking down, against the wall.

She can't imagine her Bubbe that way, hanging on the wall like a painting, death in her eyes.

She does not feel like crying, which makes her feel sad. It does not seem real—she still has Bubbe's email in her in-box. She had wanted to say other things, but she is not sure what they were.

She had told her she loved her. It was, maybe, enough.

She hears the door open, her mother's big footsteps in the kitchen, then the footsteps into her mother's room.

Abby puts on a robe and goes downstairs. She knocks on her mother's door.

Abby's mother is lying on her bed, facedown, crying.

"Mom," she says, and sits on the edge of her mother's bed.

Her mother is sobbing.

"I'm sorry, Mom," she says, not touching her, just watching her back heave up and down.

Abby's mother turns her head. Her makeup is all over. Her lipstick is smeared on her face.

"I'm fine," her mother says.

"When are we leaving?" Abby asks.

"For where?" her mother says, sitting up, blowing her nose.

"For—" Abby begins, then stops, looking at her mother's blank, streaked face. Her mother does not know. Her father has not yet reached her. Her mother has been crying for another reason: she has been crying because of what Abby has done.

She does not want her mother to die.

"Mom," she says, and puts her arms around her. Her mother begins her same heaving again.

"Mom," she says, but she does not want to tell her now. She has already been the bad news; she does not want to give her more of it.

She wishes she were bigger than her mother, and could hold her in her arms, tell her that things would be OK, break the news and then let the yolk of her mother spill all over her.

Her mother takes her head away and gets another tissue. She blows her nose.

She looks small. Her shoulders are hunched over. Abby will never be like that, she thinks. She sits up straight.

Abby doesn't want the phone to ring. She wants to keep her mother in the womb of their house. She wants to seal the house shut with silver tape and pad the walls in white leather. She wants to unplug the phones, throw out the furniture, and run from room to room.

Abby watches her mother wipe her face again. Her mother's veiny hand takes her own, smooth one.

Abby watches as her mother tries to smile.

"It's going to be OK," her mother says.

Abby looks past her mother's fake-smiling face, out the window to the gray day, the bare branches, the world outside their home. It is a day that won't stop ticking, like every other day. It is a day going on without her, only not like when she was blacked out. That time she has given away, given to Jorgen to keep in a safe place that she never wants to see.

She had not been in the right place for dying then. No one was holding her hand.

She is glad her father was with his mother, holding her hand.

She squeezes her own mother's hand, but not too hard.

She will not tell her mother, she will let the phone ring. She will watch her mother hear the news.

She will not tell her mother, whatever she knows. Jorgen will keep his story locked in a box in the basement.

She will watch her mother's eyes register death. She will watch her mother crumple more.

Then she will hold her again, make her a sandwich, cover her with a blanket, drive if she has to.

She will do all this, she thinks. Then the phone rings.

She watches her mother pick it up. She can hear her father's voice on the other line. Abby steadies herself, squares her shoulders. She is ready to take her mother's fall.

Abby watches her mother nod, listens to her say, "Yes, yes, I'm so sorry, honey, are you OK?" She watches her mother wipe her eyes again.

"Yes, I'll pack your suit."

She can hear more sounds from the phone, from her father's side, a rasping.

"Baby," her mother says. "I'm so sorry . . . It's going to be OK."

She watches her mother say "Shhh . . . shhhh," hushing her father until the noise on the other end comes back again in words.

"Yes," she says, and hangs up.

Her mother is clear-eyed, looking straight at her. She is sitting up tall. She takes Abby's hands.

"I have something to tell you," she says.

Abby looks past her mother again, out the window, where games are being played. People are driving around without her. Boys are kissing too hard.

There are teams of people working. There are people flying overseas. There is her father, out there, alone and crying. There is no one to hold him; his mother is dead.

Abby looks back at her mother, then to the print on the wall of the man handing out the world. It always looks to Abby like there is a smirk on his face, as if to say, *Take this off my hands, please* and at the same time, *Thank God it's no longer mine.*

Abby feels her mother's hands. They are softer than her own, but bony and firm.

She looks back at her mother, dry-eyed, ready, and waits for her to tell her what she already knows.

44.

Livia lies on her mother-in-law's guest room bed. The pillows are silky; the bed is firm. There are heavy curtains covering the windows. Livia is tired from driving.

She can hear Abby and Jeffrey in the den, watching TV. There is a vent between the rooms, but she does not hear them speaking. They are like that, not having to talk. Livia closes her eyes and tries to focus inside, away from the TV noise.

They got in just a few hours ago. The drive felt long. Abby had fallen asleep, and Livia had been on and off the phone with Jeffrey. His voice had sounded strained, but then jumped into a different tone, his usual tone, when he began to get into the specifics of the funeral.

Hearing him talk about the details (the synagogue, the funeral home, etc.) made her think that it was good that there was all this arranging to do when someone died. It was important to get your head out of the mess of death. Practical things, she thought. That was good for Jeffrey.

Livia opens her eyes and looks over to the guest room bureau. On top are pictures of her and Jeffrey, back when Abby was first born and Livia had gotten an awful perm. There is her wedding picture, and a picture of Headie and Allen on their honeymoon on the beach.

Headie is wearing a hat in the picture. She looks cute. It hits Livia, suddenly (again): Headie is dead.

This is good, this feeling. She was worried she would not feel this. At her own parents' funerals, she had not felt the way she was supposed to. For both her mother's and her father's, she and her brother had split the responsibilities. Even though it was most likely Rich's wife who did most of his calls, it had worked out well enough. It would have been a good distraction if Livia had felt the way she was supposed to.

But she did not feel that way until later. Not like Abby. In the car, on the way up, she saw Abby wiping tears from her cheeks.

Livia breathes in the smell of the pillows. The house has a certain odor; it is familiar and homey, but also moldy with a hint of urine. It is stale but not without air.

The last time they were here, earlier in the summer, Headie had cooked her regular dishes for dinner the first night. They had gone out to Harry's restaurant, overlooking a golf course, for a steak dinner the second. They went to synagogue with Millie. They ate lunch at her house.

It was the usual. Livia snuck off to eat in the afternoon, then came back and took a nap. They all sat in the living room and talked about nothing she could remember now. They talked about chopped liver, maybe. Nothing worth remembering.

Even though she hated Allen, it was somehow more exciting to visit when he was still alive. Livia was ready for a fight before she got there, and each time Jeffrey would have to calm her down before they went inside.

Livia did not miss Allen, but without him, Headie was different. Less talkative, maybe. She seemed to move less.

It makes her wonder what Jeffrey would be like without her. Just a few hours ago, when she and Abby walked through the back door of her mother-in-law's house, Jeffrey looked thin, unshaven, his hug softer than usual, his eyes red.

Without her, he seemed different. It had only been a couple of days.

Getting out of the car, Livia watched as Jeffrey hugged Abby. It looked like there were tears in her eyes. Jeffrey was quiet and said nothing to either of them— he did not ask about the drive, or ask about Abby as they walked inside the house.

It was quiet, still, when they got to the kitchen. Abby left the room and Livia sat down at the table while Jeffrey took their bags back to the bedrooms.

Livia noticed Headie's unplugged computer—it was newer, nicer than hers—its light still blinking, on the floor. She thought about Headie, tried to imagine her typing, her old hands, that wedding ring that seemed to have been sealed around the swelling tree trunk of her finger.

From the guest room, Livia can hear them talking. She wonders what her daughter and husband are saying. Jeffrey is probably telling Abby something that he wouldn't tell her. It makes her want to cry, thinking this.

But she does not want to cry for the wrong reasons. She is saving her crying for Headie. She can hear Abby saying, "I'm going for a walk," the back door slamming.

Livia wonders how often her daughter is smoking now. It has been only a few hours since Livia pulled into the parking lot of The Gap on their way up and Abby had her last "walk."

At The Gap, Livia had planned on going to the snack machines to get a bunch of chips, walking behind the building and eating them quickly without even waking Abby. She could just leave her in the car, she figured, run out and eat, then get back in without her knowing.

She also thought about writing Abby a note so that she didn't get scared if she did wake up. She even searched in her pocketbook for a pen. But then she looked at her daughter again. She was so beautiful, sleeping. Livia leaned over, closer, to see where Abby had plucked her eyebrows. She looked pale.

Instead, she changed her mind and reached over, softly touching her daughter's arm. She did not want to leave her there alone, she realized. Something could happen. And what if she was still sick from the alcohol?

Livia had watched her daughter open her eyes. She realized she had been holding her breath.

"We're at The Gap," Livia said. "Do you have to go?"

Abby told her she was going for a walk, and Livia was relieved. They both got out of the car and Livia went toward the bathroom. She watched Abby walk away in the opposite direction, and when she was sure she wasn't looking, she quickly doubled back to the snack machines (they had put in a few new ones—she bought four bags of chips and a Coke), then to the back entrance, already eating. She looked at her watch while opening the door, then looked down when she heard people talking. She ate fast and did not want people to watch her. She began to hiccup—too fast. She looked below where families were walking on the edge of the river. The hill was steep.

She squatted and looked farther down, and then she saw it: smoke coming from behind a tree. She saw her daughter's profile peek out—her navy sweatshirt. She watched her daughter's lips surround the cigarette, then exhale a long, full stream of smoke.

Livia kept eating, watching her daughter breathe in and out. She wondered if Abby knew about Simone. She was almost sure Chess had not seen them—there was no way—but what if she was wrong. She realized that she was timing her eating with her daughter's cigarette: it was getting close to the end, she had to eat faster.

Livia finished her last chip and walked toward the parking lot, imagining what her daughter would think of her if she knew. If her daughter thought she was a lesbian, her anger would make sense. She would be mad at her for hurting her father. It was Chess's fault.

She got in the car and looked at her phone. She dialed SIMONES HOME on her cell phone, thought about changing her voice, but then didn't have to. Chess answered and said "Hello."

"This is Abby's mother," she said.

"Hi," the boy's voice said back again.

"I need you to stay away from my daughter," she said.

"Why?" he asked. His voice seemed surprised. It seemed sincere.

Livia immediately regretted it. He sounded hurt; he didn't know. He was up in his room with loud music. He had seen nothing. Now she was sure.

"I mean, I just want you to watch out for her, OK?" she said, changing her voice, sounding kinder, softer, maybe like someone's mother.

"OK," he said. "I do."

Suddenly Abby opened the passenger door. Livia had not been paying attention—where had she been looking? She was facing straight ahead. Livia quickly hung up the phone, and Abby shut the door behind her. She did not look at her daughter, just smelled her. She started the car; she did not like the smell. She opened the windows. Her daughter needed fresh air.

And now Abby is leaving to smoke again outside Headie's house. Livia does not know how someone could have the energy to stop her. She gets up and goes into the kitchen where Jeffrey is and sits across from him in his mother's old chair.

Livia looks into her husband's eyes and watches him look away. When they were first married she couldn't imagine not knowing him the way she does not know him now.

"Do you want me to do something?" she asks.

Jeffrey puts his hands behind his head and leans back, as if challenging her.

"Like what?" he says.

"I don't know," Livia says. "Whatever it is . . . whatever you want."

"No," Jeffrey says. "You can't do anything."

She was expecting him to tell her she could organize the flowers, or call a caterer or a rabbi. She was sure he would tell her he needed help with something. She is ready to do it. She did not expect this.

It is because she was on the verge, on the edge of her seat, above a ravine where she could have fallen down in the gap of a river and she had not. She had gone on, and here she was. She had kissed a woman, been rejected, watched her daughter almost die. She had done all of this alone. And now she is here, his wife, and she is ready.

"But I want to do something," she says, leaning over and touching his thigh.

Jeffrey suddenly stands up, goes to the fridge, opens it, then turns back around.

"But it's not about you!" he shouts, his face red. "It's not about what you want!"

Livia feels herself getting ready to cry. He has not yelled at her like this in years. It feels strange, but not terrible. It is a feeling almost of excitement. A feeling she felt before, years ago, in this very house.

It has been ages since he screamed at her, since before the attempt. It was back before the au pairs, when there was only Jeffrey, herself, and Abby. She remembers Abby asking, right before their first au pair came, "But why do we have to have more people? Why can't we just stay the original family?"

This is the old feeling, but Livia does not feel like yelling back. Not the way she used to, crying and screaming, breaking pictures out of their frames, pulling sheets off the beds. She looks at her husband, who seems to be waiting to hear her.

Livia exhales, gets up, and walks to him. She does not wait for him to envelop her, to kiss her on the forehead. Instead she opens her arms and pulls him to her. She lets him lean his tall head against her shoulder. She says to him, "Here," and then says nothing else. She does not move. It is not about her.

Back in the guest room, Livia lies down again. She sees that the light is on in the closet. It is seeping out, now that it is getting darker. She can still see the pictures on the bureau, faintly. She tries to remember when she saw Headie in that great white hat she is wearing in the photo. Maybe she still has it.

When Livia was younger, thinner, Headie would open up her closet and give her her old clothes. Some were terrible, but every once in awhile she would pull out something vintage and fun. Livia loved when Headie did this. Allen and Jeffrey would always be somewhere else, and it would just be her and Headie, alone, in her bedroom closet, or this guest room's closet, or sometimes even in the basement where she stored things in big plastic hanging bags. It was another way Headie was so different from her own mother, who was not someone who liked to share.

It was true that sometimes Headie was harsh. She would tell her if something did not look good. Still, she noticed Livia, appreciated her, looked at her in the mirror from behind and pulled down her skirt, or pulled the waist in the back, to show her how she might look better.

Livia has a flash of a photograph, or maybe just a memory, of her mother looking at herself in the mirror and crying. No, it couldn't be a photograph. Perhaps Livia had been spying. But that seems strange.

Livia stretches and yawns, then turns on the nightstand light and opens the closet. Inside are all the clothes she has never taken. Some have been there forever (she remembers one brown suit that Headie was always trying to get rid of), next to all the shoes that never fit (Headie's feet were size 6; Livia is a size 10).

Livia looks up at the old hatboxes from the store Headie worked at. She takes one down, hoping it is the white hat in the picture. Not that it would fit her (that was another thing Headie could never pass on: Livia's head was much bigger than her mother-in-law's), but maybe, she thought, for Abby.

Inside is an old ugly brown hat, a man's hat, not something she can remember Allen wearing. Livia reaches up and takes down another box. Inside is a fur hat, a woman's hat, nothing Abby would want.

Livia pulls down some sweaters, then begins to go through the hanging clothes. They will have to pack this all up soon, give it to Goodwill or the synagogue. She figures she should go through it all at least once before they do. Perhaps there will be a surprise. Once she found a gold charm of a tiny girl's silhouette in one of the shirt pockets that Headie had given her. It is like a treasure hunt.

Livia combs through the rack (a shirt that might be OK, slacks, slacks, slacks that no one would want, an eighties-style dress). She stops at a pink garment bag, then opens it, wondering if it might be Headie's old wedding dress.

Livia unzips the bag and finds another plastic bag, this time see-through, as if Headie just pulled a garbage bag over it. She takes this off the hanger too, and beneath it sees a nightgown with a note on an index card pinned to it.

BURY ME IN THIS! it says.

45.

Abby sits in her Bubbe's TV room with her father. She knows she smells like smoke so she tries not to sit too close. She rubbed evergreen needles on her fingers before coming in, like she always does with Jenna, but she is not sure this really works.

Abby's father looks tired, and she does not want him to smell her. They watch the local news and Abby does not change the channel.

Her father has not said anything about the Pep Rally, or the fact that this is her first day of suspension. Instead he gave her a hug when she came in, and it looked like he might have been crying. This is impossible to imagine, and makes Abby feel dizzy, like she felt the other day in the woods watching the game.

Abby checks her phone to see if anyone has texted her, but her screen has been blank since Jenna on the bleachers. Abby likes being suspended, likes being in her grandmother's house. It is like vacation, sort of. Perhaps things will be different if she tells everyone her grandmother died.

Abby looks across the room at the two prints of ferns on the wall. She wonders if this is something her Bubbe chose to put up. It seems more like Grandpa Allen's idea. She cannot imagine her Bubbe even saying the word "fern."

Abby remembers her mother talking once when she was little, in the car on the ride home from a visit, about how Allen was unbearable. She used that word: unbearable. Abby pretended to sleep in the back seat so her mother would talk more freely. She liked to hear what was said when her parents were alone, without her, but usually it was only her mother talking.

Still, it was fascinating, and on long car rides anywhere, Abby would keep her eyes closed for as long as she could. Surprisingly, what they said was not so different from what she heard them say when she was awake. It made her feel strange to think that this was it: this was her parents' marriage.

Abby looks over at her father. He is watching a commercial about wood polish.

Seeing him wrapped up in the commercial, seemingly so interested, makes her suddenly sad.

As soon as the commercials are over, Abby's father gets up and turns off the TV. She watches him sit down next to her, then turn to her. He is so serious, she has to stop herself from smirking.

"You know, my mom was a really good mother," he says.

Abby is surprised. She does not know what to say to this. She was a good Bubbe.

"Oh," she says.

"She was strong and got what she wanted," he says. "And she was loving and caring. I want you to remember that."

"I will," Abby says, looking at her father. "I promise."

"And you know, she wasn't always perfect," he goes on, "but she tried her best. That is what's important."

Abby wonders if her father is trying to teach her a lesson. It is not his usual tone.

"And she loved you very much," he says.

Abby looks away, toward the ferns on the wall. It is too much. He is not trying to tell her anything, she realizes. It is like he is talking to himself, and she wishes he would stop.

She wants to hug him, but she is scared he will cry. She is scared, too, that she will cry. She is scared they will not stop crying.

Abby hears her mother's footsteps coming down the hall. She opens the door without knocking, and stands in front of them, holding what looks like a nightgown in front of her.

It looks funny, like a doll's, so small against her mother's tall frame.

"Look what I found," her mother says, leaning over the two of them and laying the nightgown gently over their knees, stretched out to its full length.

She points to a note on the collar.

BURY ME IN THIS! it says.

It strikes Abby as funny, but she stops herself from smiling when she looks at her father, who is not smiling at all. He is touching the note, then feeling the fabric of the collar.

"I guess we know what to dress her in," her mother says.

It is almost like a person, Abby thinks, the way the nightgown is stretched out across their legs.

A vision of her Bubbe, laid out somewhere, comes to her. She wonders if she is naked on a table, or already dressed in something else, in a coffin. The funeral is tomorrow. They must be getting her ready, she thinks.

"I already gave them a suit for her," her father says quietly. He seems so tired.

"We can drop it off. I'll call them. I'm sure it's not too late," Livia says, picking up the nightgown again. "Where's the number for the funeral home?"

Abby gets up and goes to the bathroom. Why an ugly nightgown? But maybe it would be comfortable . . . Maybe Bubbe thought about death like sleep. Death, like blacking out in the woods while the football boys shouted their names. First you are there, breathing. Then you are nowhere.

Abby is here, sitting on the toilet, peeing, then looking at herself in the mirror. She looks at her eyebrows; they need to be plucked again but she is not sure she brought her tweezers. She looks at her upper lip; there is very little hair.

She looks closer, at her skin. She sticks her lips out and wonders who she has kissed.

She wonders if she kissed Chess. She wonders where she kissed Alec. Had she tried to kiss Jenna? Does everyone know? She looks at her eyes, again, then puckers her lips. She thinks that this is what whoever kissed her saw before they kissed her. They saw her this close, then closed their eyes. Up this close, and she was kissable.

"Let's go!" she hears her mother yell. "They need the nightgown now."

Abby un-purses her lips, leaves the bathroom, and gets her jacket. Her parents are already out the door.

"I'll drive," her mother says. Abby watches her father say nothing and slump down in the passenger seat. Abby gets in the back, like always.

Outside it is gray. While her mother drives, she watches the houses go by. It is hard to imagine the neighborhood on a sunny day.

It seems depressing in a way she hadn't seen before. All those years coming up, just lying down in the backseat, or getting up to sit, but not seeing what she sees now. A sad town. Near where her father grew up. A coal town, he had once told her, just like his own.

She thinks how her Bubbe always lived in towns like this. Towns with hard soil and dirty air. Towns with limits. She had heard her mother once say that if she had lived in a different era, her mother-in-law would have made a good lawyer.

But she had not been a lawyer. She had made her son into one, Abby thought. She wondered what her parents were making her into.

The nightgown is hung up next to her in the backseat, wrapped in clear plastic. She can see the note still safety-pinned inside.

The note seems too private, so she reaches in the bag and unpins it. She does not want the funeral director to see it. She imagines a fat man in a suit unpinning it himself and smiling.

She holds the note and pin in her hand, and smoothes down the front of the bag. She looks at the note again. Close up, she can see that the words are a bit faded. She wonders how long it has hung in Bubbe's closet like this and when it became special; if, at one point, it was just a nightgown folded up in a drawer among others before it was singled out.

Abby turns the paper over. There is small lettering, a name, written tiny in unsteady script: Jeffrey Goldstein, it says, in darker blue—as if it was written more recently. No, not her father's name.

She looks at it and wonders if it is like a wish. A wish, like "Abby Johnson." A wish, she thinks, like she hadn't been at Pep Rally. A wish like a secret sewn into a leaf that was left by the Living Room telling all the things she's done wrong.

A wish that she had stopped her mother, had broken down the door, had stolen the pills they found inside her.

A wish like her grandmother's: to change things. To sum her life up, to make her son part of the man she loved.

Her father would be furious if he saw this. Abby puts the paper in her pocket for now. It is a note for another time. Her mother is talking, she realizes, quietly. She had not been paying attention. She leans forward.

Her father is speaking softly, in full sentences. He is saying something that is hard for her to hear. She leans closer and sees her mother's hands: one on the steering wheel, the other resting on her father's leg.

She watches her father take her mother's fingers.

Abby lies back down on the seat, pulling her legs up so she can fit her whole body across. She can hear her mother begin to talk again, but it is like she is whispering; Abby cannot hear what she is saying. She closes her eyes, and listens instead to the sound of the road beneath them, the raindrops on the windows, the circulating air. She imagines herself in a black box, under covers, in bed, at home.

Below her, she imagines Jorgen banging pans in the kitchen. She imagines her mother, walking heavily between floors. She imagines her father falling asleep next to her on the couch.

She imagines going out on her roof. Soon it will get colder, and it will be harder for her to sit out there at night.

If no one asks for it, if no one notices, she will put her Bubbe's note in one of her shoeboxes, next to her cigarettes. If no one wants it, then she will see it each time she smokes. If no one ever says anything, then she won't either.

She will look at her Bubbe's note. Jeffrey Goldstein, she thinks. Abby Goldstein, she thinks. She is glad she is a Schecter.

Unattached to anything, she thinks now, the paper hiding in her pocket. She could burn it, but she won't.

"Jeffrey Goldstein" makes her think of Grandpa Allen and his bald head. He was childless. Abby wondered if he had wanted one.

One child, like herself. Perhaps he wanted her father.

Abby feels the car slowing down again. She opens her eyes and looks in the space between the two front seats. There, her parents' hands are holding each other.

There is room enough for her to reach through, to put her own hand on top, to fill the space.

She reaches out her hand and looks at it, smooth and alone. She thinks about how soon she will need gloves, how her parents' hands look warm, how she has never seen them hold hands before.

She thinks about all the things her hands have done without them; how after they had her, she was alone.

It is strange to think of that, and to think of all the people a person can touch. To think how their touches rub off on you, even when they are no longer touching.

Abby feels the car stop and realizes she has closed her eyes. She opens them, and looks again at the front seat, at the space. There they are, their hands still holding.

Abby closes her eyes again, like she used to do, and pretends to be asleep.

She listens to the car wind down and lets her parents touch.

Acknowledgments

I am grateful to the following people, without whom this book would not have come to fruition.

My editor, Joanna Yas, for her patience, intelligence, sense of humor, and gentle guidance.

My agent, Emilie Stewart, for her persistence, enthusiasm, and belief in my work.

And to my family, for being there.